The Vampire Next Door

Natalie Vivien and Bridget Essex

The Vampire Next Door

Books by Natalie Vivien

Heart-Shaped Box
French Lessons
Drawn to You
Love Stories
The Ghost of a Chance
Falling for Hope
The Thousand Mile Love Story
For the Love of Indiana

Books by Bridget Essex

A Wolf for Valentine's Day
A Wolf for the Holidays
Don't Say Goodbye
Forever and a Knight
A Knight to Remember
Wolf Town
Dark Angel
Big, Bad Wolf
The Protector (Lone Wolf, Book 1)
Meeting Eternity: The Sullivan Vampires, Vol. 1

The Vampire Next Door

About the Authors

Natalie Vivien and Bridget Essex write love stories, because they live a love story that inspires them every day. Together for over a decade, married for over eight years, they are madly and passionately in love, and build a good, cozy life together with several fur babies who get away with murder because they're so adorable.

Natalie and Bridget founded Rose and Star Press in 2014, a publisher of lesbian romance and fiction of distinction. Lesbian romance is their life's work, and they hope very much that you enjoyed *The Vampire Next Door*, the first book that they wrote *together*.

Learn more about Natalie at **http://natalievivien.wordpress.com** or send her an email at **miss.natalie.vivien@gmail.com**. Learn more about Bridget at **http://bridgetessex.wordpress.com** or email her at **bridgetessexauthor@gmail.com**.

Learn more about Rose and Star Press, publishers of lesbian romance and fiction of distinction, at
http:///www.LesbianRomance.org

The Vampire Next Door
Copyright © 2015 Natalie Vivien and Bridget Essex
All Rights Reserved
Published by Rose and Star Press
First edition, April 2015

This is a work of fiction. Names, characters, places and incidents either are products of the author's imagination or are used fictitiously. Any resemblance to actual events or locales or persons, living or dead, is entirely coincidental.

This book, or parts thereof, may not be reproduced without written permission.

ISBN: 150521470X
ISBN-13: 978-1505214703

The Vampire Next Door

The Vampire Next Door

Chapter One: The Woman with Silver Eyes

"I'm sorry, Mr. Hanover, but I can assure you that William Shakespeare did *not* write *Huckleberry Finn*," I sigh into my cell phone.

"Ha!" Azure spins around to face me, gaping. She points at the phone gripped in my hand and mouths, *Are you kidding me?* Her dark green eyes roll heavenward.

I know, I mouth back, listening halfheartedly to the man chattering on the line. Mr. Hanover is an antique book collector, but he's not a book *reader*. He's rich, though, and he's one of our regular suppliers, so I don't want to insult him—if I can help it. Still...I don't want to insult Mr. Shakespeare or Mr. Twain, either.

"Listen, Mr. Hanover, why don't you bring your book into the store? I'll look it over and give it an appraisal. Even if it's a fake—"

"It is *not* a fake," he insists in his gruff, no-nonsense voice. Mr. Hanover sounds remarkably like a walrus, and, with his thick mustache and penchant for wrinkly brown suits, he looks a bit like one, too.

Azure and I have this habit of comparing

our regulars to animals. Abigail Rogers resembles a high-strung hare; Lewis Oliver, with his cowlick and colorful ties, a peacock. When you work in a store specializing in rare books and average two live customers per day, you've got to amuse yourself somehow. Sure, I love alphabetizing as much as the next Virgo, but even obsessive organizing gets a little dull after a ten-hour shift.

Mr. Hanover clears his throat. "I have been collecting first editions for more decades than you've been *alive*, Miss Banks—"

"*Ms.*, please," I interrupt him, drawing a deep breath into my lungs. I shove a red leather-bound, nineteenth-century copy of *The Three Musketeers* onto a shelf, between *The Man in the Iron Mask* and *Twenty Years After*.

"Ms. Banks. And I think I know a thing or two about authenticity and forgery. Now, if you aren't interested in purchasing this book from me, I'll take it over to Palmer's on Fourth. I'm sure Randolph Palmer would appreciate my business—"

"I'm sure he would. In fact, I *insist* that you take the book to Randolph Palmer. Go on. Please. With my blessing."

A pause. Then Mr. Hanover says, in a low, level tone, "I don't like your attitude, Miss Banks."

"*Ms.* Banks."

Azure cackles, giving me a double

thumbs-up.

"All right, then." Mr. Hanover harrumphs into the receiver. "Perhaps it *is* time for me to take my business elsewhere. Banks' Books hasn't been the same since you took over ownership, you know. Your mother handled herself with decorum. As any *proper* lady should. She was never cross or contrary with me. Lana never dared accuse me of selling a counterfeit book."

Of course she didn't, I think, dispirited, as I shelf an illustrated copy of *Little Women*.

My mother—Lana Banks—now retired and enjoying a sizzling south Florida summer, is a book lover and a people-pleaser but no businesswoman. After Dad died, he left the store to her in his will, despite their being long divorced. Out of guilt or curiosity (Mom will try anything once), she managed the bookstore to the best of her ability, but her lack of general business sense caused us to slide, slowly but surely, into the red. When I finished up my Masters in Business and took over store operation three years ago, we were *this close* to declaring bankruptcy.

Thanks to some lucky acquisitions from estate sales and the addition of an Internet store, Banks' Books is now gasping towards profitability...more or less. If I lose any more key suppliers, though—Mr. Hanover, for all of his ignorance, does have connections in the antique books world—I might not ever be able to give Azure and David the raises they deserve. I...might not be able to pay my mortgage.

And I *definitely* won't be able to replace my lemon of a car. My ancient, mustard-yellow Cavalier has 250,000 miles on it, no hubcaps, and an unfortunate habit of stalling out in intersections, at stop signs, and—most often—in my driveway. Originally, when I bought the car from my cousin Georgie for a thousand bucks, I named it Diva Dijon, but I've since decided that it doesn't deserve such a classy name. Or a feminine gender identity.

So Colonel Mustard it is.

"I'm not accusing you of anything, Mr. Hanover," I murmur into my cell phone, walking to the end of the aisle, rounding the desk, and sliding into the chair behind the old iron cash register. I slip my feet out of my heels and massage my pounding temples. Then I glance up at the wall clock: twenty minutes until closing.

Thank God.

It's been a long, *long* day.

"As I told you," I say, striving to sound pleasant despite my clenched teeth, "if you'd like me to appraise the book, I'm more than willing to do so, but I just have to warn you that—"

"But nothing, *Ms.* Banks. Palmer will do right by me. If *you're* interested in my book, you'll have to buy it from *him*."

I sigh, raking a hand back through my blonde tangles. I woke up groggy and late this morning, so I couldn't be bothered to run a brush through my hair. I'm kind of surprised that I arrived fully clothed.

"Tell your mother I send my regards. And my sympathy for the impending bankruptcy of her store. Good-bye."

"Good-bye, Mr. Hanover," I say flatly, pressing the *end* button on my phone. Then I make a pathetic whining sound and bang my head against the cash register—repeatedly. When my hair finally gets caught in the typewriter-like keys and I signal an SOS with my arm, Azure—patient, purple-mohawked Azure—drops the stack of books she was sorting and helps me pull the long strands free.

"Hey, I know he was a regular supplier and everything, but do you *really* want to do business with a guy who confuses Mark *Twain* with William *Shakespeare*? That's got to be, like, a literary felony." Azure smooths a swath of tangles back from my forehead. "Even schoolkids know that Mark Twain wrote *Huckleberry Finn*."

I frown. "Yeah, but I was kind of rude."

"Mr. *Hanover* is rude—*and* a misogynist. I heard him, insinuating that you don't know what you're talking about. You silly little *woman*, you." Azure rolls her eyes again. "Do you remember that time he told you you were a dead ringer for some silent film starlet, and that you were too pretty to work around books?"

I grimace.

"Plus, he's technologically illiterate. Anyone could Google what you told him in two seconds." Azure's lips curl up into a wicked smile. "God, I'd pay big bucks to overhear his conversation with Palmer."

I shake my head. "Randolph's smart. If he finds out that Mr. Hanover has dissolved his relationship with my store, he'll pounce on the opportunity to win his loyalty. Even if it means purchasing a counterfeit antique."

Azure shrugs and sighs, leaning against the counter as I tuck some strands of hair behind my ear and straighten a stack of books beside the register. "Anyway—" I begin to tell her, but I'm interrupted.

The front door of Banks' Books jangles open, and Azure and I look up, surprised. It's nearly closing time; we don't often get walk-ins on Wednesday nights.

A woman with china-smooth skin and wavy red hair steps into the store, her high-heeled boots clicking over the worn floorboards. I part my lips to call out a greeting, but my vocal chords refuse to cooperate: I'm frozen in place, still and speechless. All I can do is look; I can't tear my eyes away... The woman is stunning—literally. Every atom in my body is dazed, startled, by the mere sight of her.

I think time has stopped ticking.

I think my heart has stopped beating.

"Wow, she's beautiful," Azure whispers.

"Yeah," I whisper back, staring. *Oh, God, I'm staring.* I blink quickly and look away, shuffling junk mail on the desktop. With shaking hands, I draw a glossy brochure out of the mess—propaganda for an organization called SANG—and pretend like I'm fascinated by it, though, frankly, the group's mantra turns my stomach: *If you're with them, you're against us.*

Despite my clumsy subterfuge, I can still glimpse our customer out of the corner of my eye. She's long and lean but somehow soft-looking. And that hair... It's shampoo commercial hair, thick and lustrous, curling loosely over her collarbones and as red as autumn leaves. She's dressed in a fitted blue pinstripe suit, and the first three buttons of her white shirt are undone, revealing a black stone pendant dangling at the base of her throat.

She might be the most beautiful woman I've ever seen.

I mean, not that beauty is everything. I've never really had a *type.*

Or...I didn't think I had a type.

Until now.

As I watch, the woman shifts her head, and her blue eyes glint silver.

15

Silver.

Oh...

Azure gives me a knowing look. My best friend is one of the most perceptive people I know; of course she noticed the silver sheen, too.

Suddenly, that Darkling song—the one that they played on the radio every half hour a couple of summers ago—starts running through my head: *And the last thing she ever saw was silver. And the last mouth she ever kissed cursed her. And the last word she ever spoke was "vampire."*

Okay.

Chances are...this woman isn't quite human.

I glance at her left wrist, but her jacket sleeves cover her arms completely, so I don't know whether she has the telltale tattoo. She looks off toward the shelves and shoves her hands deep into her pockets.

Heart skipping, I swallow and shake my messy hair behind my shoulders. *Get a grip, Courtney. You've dealt with vampires before.*

One of the store's most loyal customers, Desmond Lennox, is a vampire; he's been patronizing our business since its inception. He knew my grandfather and used to play golf with him on the weekends—and, if photographs are any indication, he's barely aged a day since.

Of course, my grandfather didn't *know* Mr. Lennox was a vampire. None of us (or very few of us) humans knew vampires existed until three years ago, when President Garcia announced that she had descended from a long line of vampires and was, in fact, a blood-drinker herself. She enacted immediate legal measures to allow other vampires to out themselves safely, and she acquired funding to open Safe Centers in every major city. The Safe Centers provide free packets of sterilized animal blood to registered vampires, thus reducing the likelihood of their contracting blood-borne diseases—or seeking human victims.

To be perfectly honest, the whole vampire thing has taken some getting used to. I grew up thinking vampires were myths, metaphors, the imaginative embodiment of humanity's fear of blood and death.

But...they're real.

And they're everywhere.

Some of them, like President Garcia and Desmond Lennox, look like elderly politicians.

And some of them, like the woman standing in my shop's doorway, are really, really, *really* hot.

There's a rumor that vampires exude a special pheromone that makes everyone who meets them want to, well, jump their bones. But the only vampires I've encountered are of the grandfatherly and/or male variety: not so tempting for a 35-year-old lesbian, preternatural pheromones notwithstanding.

This woman, though...

"Welcome to Banks' Books," I force out. My voice is shaky, along with my knees, and I'm not sure whether that's because I'm talking to a vampire who happens to be beautiful, or a beautiful woman who happens to be a vampire. Either way, I'm feeling inappropriate *stirrings* in two or three inappropriate places.

I chew on my bottom lip.

The woman turns her head and meets my gaze. "Oh, hello," she says, smiling. My stomach flip-flops, and I smile back. "Gorgeous shop," she murmurs, her voice low, throaty, causing me to shiver as I find myself leaning towards her. "I love that old book smell." Her mouth, turning up at the corners, draws my eye. "It reminds me of a bookstore in Paris — Shakespeare and Company. Have you ever been there?"

I shake my head.

Her eyes widen. "You ought to go someday. The place is steeped in literary history..." She watches me for a moment. Then she glances at the shelves again and moves further into the shop. "Well, I'm new to the neighborhood, so I haven't been in here before. I was wondering if you could help me—"

"That's why we're here!" Azure steps out from behind the desk and passes a hand over the top of her mohawk. It's a nervous habit of hers — and a telling sign. Whenever she's attracted to a woman, she starts fussing with her hair. She also tends to talk superfast: "Are you a collector? Were you looking for something specific? Or did you want to find a gift, maybe? We have some gift baskets on the table by the window."

"No, I..." The woman moves further into the store, pausing before Azure and then casting a friendly glance toward me. Her eyes are pale and blue, though they gleam silver, like mirrors, whenever light shimmers over their surface. "I have an odd request." She has the shadow of an accent, I realize then, but I can't place it. French? She did mention Paris...

"Well, you're in luck. We specialize in odd." Azure winks and holds out her hand. "I'm Azure Skye, and this is my boss, Courtney Banks."

"Oh, you're the owner?" The woman shakes Azure's hand distractedly before moving past her and approaching me at the register. I see Azure's shoulders sink. She's always had a thing for redheads. Her last girlfriend, Billie, was a redhead. But Billie was short, and our unexpected customer is tall—taller than Azure, and as tall as me. I take after my dad in the height department, though our similarities, admittedly, stop there. He was obsessed with sports—everything from golf to football to Foosball—and my pursuits have always been of the nose-in-a-book variety.

"Yes," I tell the woman, straightening my

shoulders. "I'm the owner."

"A co-worker of mine recommended your store." Her eyes glint. "He said you've got the best rare books collection in Cincinnati."

I blush. Then, mortified over the fact that I've blushed, I clear my throat, straighten my back and go into full-on entrepreneur mode. When panicked/flailing/freaking out, I tend to talk shop—excessively. "Banks' Books has been around for three generations. We've amassed our stock over the course of a hundred years, so we have a wide network of contacts in the book world."

"A hundred years, huh?"

"Yeah..." I lick my lips. God, what am I doing? I sound like a salesman—or a fact-spouting robot. In an effort to appear more relaxed, I place my elbows on the top of the desk and rest my chin on my hands. But the desk is too low. I feel awkward and look ridiculous. One of my elbows slips out from beneath me, and I fall forward a little, then catch myself and straighten again.

Robo Courtney will have to do.

"If you're searching for a particular book, we'll make every attempt to locate it for you, either here in the store, online, or through our liaisons."

The woman's mouth slants upward on one side, and I catch myself staring again... She has an amazing mouth. Somehow she can smile ironically and warmly, all at once. "Like I said, it's an odd request. As far as I know, the book I want doesn't even exist."

I lift a brow. Okay, now I'm curious. There's nothing I love more than a literary challenge. I grab my cell phone; then I move around the desk and lean against the nearest row of shelves. "Would this imaginary book be fiction or non-fiction?" I ask, enabling the store catalog app on my phone, a searchable database of our in-stock inventory.

"Non-fiction," she says, then laughs. "Though most of my colleagues would beg to differ. Tell me, Ms. Banks"—she steps close, tilting her head down so that she gazes at me through long lashes—"what do you know about alchemy?" Her sterling eyes flash.

"Um, alchemy?" Caught off guard by the sight of my reflection in her gaze—*and the last thing she ever saw was silver*—I smile uncertainly and shake my head. "Not much. Sorry."

"We've got some books about Robert Boyle in the science aisle, and I just shelved a Philosopher's Stone pamphlet under folklore," Azure says brightly, appearing at my side. "It's a facsimile, though, not an original."

"Hmm." The woman nods thoughtfully. "That's a start. But I'm more interested in transmutation."

I lift my brow again. "You mean, like...changing lead to gold?"

"Something like that." A slow grin. Her eyes slide over me, pausing when they reach my lips. I feel my own mouth open, and I'm staring at her lips, too, at the pointed teeth revealed as her teasing smile slowly widens. By arousal or instinct, my heartbeat speeds up; my breathing goes shallow...

I want to run from her.
I want to kiss her.

God, Courtney, you have a girlfriend. A small but crucial fact I've blissfully and uncharacteristically ignored since this woman stepped through the door.

It's the pheromone. It's *got* to be the pheromone...

She turns toward Azure. "Can you show me where the Boyle books are?"

"Absolutely!"

Chatty Azure leads the woman between the shelves, leaving me alone with my wobbly knees and achy chest. I stagger behind the desk and busy myself by shoving the junk mail into the shredder and checking the store's email account on my laptop. There are three requests for books we already have in stock. I respond to each message, but I'm so distracted that I misspell my own name in one of the replies, and in another, I catch myself writing *vampire* in the place of *acquire* — which doesn't even make *sense*.

By the time Azure reappears, I've calmed my nerves and cold-showered my hormones —

more or less. But my voice is unnaturally high when I ask, "Any luck?"

The woman shakes her head; her red waves shine like copper beneath the store's amber-colored lamplight. "Sadly, no."

"Oh. Well, I'm sorry, Ms.—"

"Máille. Valeria Máille. Call me Lare. And don't apologize, Ms. Banks." Her glance, with its startling silver, holds me in place.

"Please," I tell her, licking my lips, "call me Courtney."

Azure shoots me a startled look. I blush again and glance down at the desk. But I got rid of the mail, so there's nothing for me to pretend to be interested in. I lift my gaze, offering Azure a pathetic, "Well, can you really blame me?" smile.

Normally, to maintain professionalism, I insist that customers refer to me by my surname only. Being a female business owner is tough enough. Allowing customers to call me Courtney opens the door to unwanted familiarity, and before you know it, they start coming up with all sorts of patronizing, cavity-inducing nicknames: sweetie, honey, sugar, cutie pie, cupcake. A guy looking for a copy of *Moby Dick* referred to me as "cupcake" once. Once. After the feminist diatribe that Azure and I subjected him to, he never dared to call me "cupcake" again. Or to come back into the store.

As Azure tells the tale, he left with his

"little Moby Dick flapping like a dead fish between his legs." In reality, he knocked over our Jane Austen display and flipped us the proverbial bird on his way out the door. (Later, Azure and I decided that the animal he most resembled was a sea cucumber.)

So my asking this customer to call me Courtney is entirely out of character. And entirely out of line.

After all (I have to remind myself *again*), I've been in a committed relationship with Mia for five months.

Guilt clenches my stomach. I shake my head and stare at the store catalog on my cell phone. "If you give me some keywords, I can perform a search of our inventory. I have access to our suppliers' inventories, too."

"Clever device." The woman smiles, resting her hands on the top of the desk. Her fingers are long, the sharp nails painted charcoal gray, almost black. "All right, then. I'm looking for anything you might find regarding the research of an ancient Roman alchemist named Maximinus. I've already sucked the Internet dry—"

I glance up, wide-eyed, and she laughs softly, offering me a sheepish smile.

"Sorry. I have a tendency towards puns." Sliding her sleeve up over her arm, she presents her wrist to me: its smooth surface is tattooed with a large black V, facing outward. Below the

V is a series of numbers—45832. Her registration number. By law, all vampires are required to have one.

"I'm sure you already guessed." She winks, and her eyes gleam, sky blue and polished silver. "But transparency is important in any relationship, don't you think?"

I nod, too flustered to respond.

This woman, this vampire—Lare—smells like sugar and lilies and sex. A quick glance at Azure tells me that she's equally smitten. But Azure's single. I, on the other hand... Self-reproach bangs around inside my chest like a pinball—remember Mia; Mia, your *girlfriend*.

I type Maximinus into the search bar on my phone's screen. "Zero results."

Lare sighs. "I expected as much. He isn't well known, even in scientific circles."

I clear my throat, exit the app, and place my cell on the desk. "Well, the next step is to send out requests to our network. Is there anything else you can tell me about this guy? Was he affiliated with anyone famous—or infamous?"

"He was a contemporary of Galileo. And his work was kind of...fringe."

I gaze at her. "Fringe?"

She shifts, ducking her head down bashfully. Adorably.

Mia, Mia, Mia, my girlfriend Mia...

"Um. Yeah. He was kind of into..." She

25

exhales and smiles, shrugging her shoulders. "Well, blood."

"Oh. Blood. Of course. I mean—" I shake my head. "Not of course. Just... Well, you're a... Sorry. That's—I shouldn't have said *of course*. I'm sure you're interested in all sorts of things besides..." I cough into my hand; my face is burning up. "You know."

But Lare laughs, leaning toward me. "I *am* interested in all sorts of things. And"—her voice lowers as her shining eyes search mine—"all sorts of people."

"Oh," I squeak.

"Oh," Azure says, running up to the desk and staring at me pointedly. "Court, it's past closing. Don't you have a movie date with Mia tonight? You know, Mia? Your girlfriend? Mia? *Remember?*"

"No." I shake my head, feeling even more flushed as Lare lifts her chin, gazing back and forth between us, looking perplexed. "I don't think—"

"You do. I'm sure you do."

Eyes narrowed, I return Azure's stare. She isn't an interfering sort of person. If she's telling me that I have a date with Mia tonight...maybe I do? I've been stressed out lately. Thanks to Randolph Palmer's new marketing campaign, our sales have slipped over the past two months, so I've been working longer hours, and Mia has been preoccupied with her position at the paper. We have short conversations on the phone, Mia sleeps at my place a couple of nights every week, but we haven't gone out in...a while.

And I haven't felt emotionally connected to her in, well, a while.

And if we scheduled a date for tonight, it slipped my mind completely.

The guilt in my gut has alchemically transmuted itself from a pinball to a bowling ball. And not a pink, glittery, seven-pound bowling bowl. It's one of those stupidly heavy bowling balls, the kind that makes you stagger as you struggle along, trying desperately to avoid dropping it on your foot...

"You're closed; I should go," Lare says. She reaches into her pocket and draws out a business card, which she presses into my hand. I shiver a little when her palm touches mine—but not because her skin is cold. It isn't.

Contrary to folklore, real vampires don't have cold skin. They do tend to be a little pale, but not pancake-makeup pale, and they can enjoy the sunshine without repercussion, so long as they wear sunglasses during the brightest hours of the afternoon to protect their sensitive eyes. Best of all, they're able to subsist on non-human (i.e. animal) blood quite comfortably.

Or so I've heard. Most of my vampire knowledge (or lack thereof) has been garnered from overheard conversations, magazine headlines, and late-night entertainment shows, embarrassingly enough.

"Give me a call if you find anything. Anytime." Lare's mouth curves up on one side, baring the tip of her right incisor. "I hardly ever sleep." She arches a brow, and her gleaming eyes sweep over me—slowly, thoughtfully. When they meet my gaze again, they look crystal blue, soft, inviting...and a little amused. She smiles, and I smile back, despite the flutter of anxiety in my stomach.

Lare turns toward Azure and offers her a small wave. "Thanks for your help."

"Sure, no problem." Azure rounds the desk to stand beside me, and we both watch as Lare leaves the store, the string of large jangling bells tied to the door pull announcing her exit.

Then, in sync, we look at each other, stare at each other, shake our heads simultaneously—in mute and mutual wonder—and then sigh.

"Did that really just happen?" Azure asks.

I bite my lip.

"You've got the hots for her, don't you, boss?"

I bite my lip harder.

Azure slings her arm around my shoulder and gives me her *Courtney, what were you thinking?* look. Then she says, black eyebrows raised high, "Courtney, what were you thinking?"

"I don't know!" I tell her, feeling my

stomach squeeze. "I don't know, all right? I just... It was so weird. And... Well, nothing *happened*. Nothing's *going* to happen. *God*, I haven't been attracted to someone like that since..." I start to say *Mia*, but I pause—because, well, I've never been attracted to anyone like *that*, not ever. It *had* to have been the pheromone... "Hey, Az, do I really have a date with Mia tonight?"

She nods, her eyes wide. "You're supposed to go the movies. Did you forget?"

"Um...yeah. I guess I did," I tell her with a sigh. "We didn't talk about it last night. Or...I don't remember talking about it. God, am I a terrible person?"

"Hey." Azure gives me a quick squeeze and then lets go. She leans against the desk, chuckling softly. "Relax. Lare threw me for a loop, too. You know what they say about vampires. They *ooze* sex appeal. They give off these, like, sexy, invisible secretions. Like they're wearing some kind of human-luring perfume. Makes sense, you know. They're at the top of the food chain. Or were, before the government got involved."

"Yeah." I frown, unconvinced, and fall into the chair. "Yeah. I guess that makes sense."

"Geez, you look beat, Court. Why don't you take off? I'll close up. No worries."

I smile at her gratefully.

When I first met Azure in a literary

criticism class, she had straight black hair and called herself Lauren Blankenship. But since then, she's undergone a personal metamorphosis, transforming—just like one of those cartoon superheroines—into purple-haired Azure Skye, local folk rock star. And part-time bookstore employee, because she doesn't earn enough from singing gigs yet to cover her bills.

"Thanks, Az. You're—" I begin, but my phone starts buzzing on the desktop.

"Don't tell me it's the Walrus again." Azure crosses her arms over her chest, obscuring the giant pink triangle on her t-shirt. "Here—let me handle him."

"No, it's Mia." I glance down at my phone, see her picture on the screen and feel another twinge of guilt. I pick it up, press *send* and say, "One second, baby," into the receiver. Then I cover up the mouthpiece with my hand and ask Azure, "Are you sure you wouldn't mind closing the store tonight?"

"Sure as the shore. Consider it done." She smiles warmly, pats my shoulder, and then shoves me—hard—off of the chair. "Go, go! Chill, unwind. Do something *shockingly* sexy. With Mia," she tells me, her lips twitching into a smile, "*not* the vampire."

"Azure, I wouldn't—"

"Kidding." She winks. "*Obviously.* Anyway, as the Bard would say: *Go, girl, seek happy nights—*"

I snort. "My idea of a *happy night* is a long, hot soak in the tub with *Jane Eyre* and a bottomless glass of wine."

Azure frowns. "Well, Mia might not appreciate your bathing with another woman—fictional or otherwise—but whatever floats your boat, Court."

"See you tomorrow, Az," I laugh. "And thanks for the favor. I owe you one."

"You don't owe me anything, boss. Except cash money. Hey, you're still coming to the music fest, right?"

I nod, grabbing my purse from a shelf under the desk. "Already bought tickets for Mia and me."

"Awesome. I think it's actually going to sell out!" With that, Azure hefts her abandoned stack of books up from the floor and disappears down the second aisle, singing softly to herself—something about *female oppression* and *diamond rings* and *dirty diapers*. She's been writing and recording her first album, *Words that Rhyme with Misogyny*, over the past couple of months, but I've never seen Azure perform on stage before; up until this point, she's forbidden me from attending her shows, insisting that she wasn't ready for peer reviews. So I've only heard snippets of her lyrics sung beneath her breath. Azure has this husky, melodic, Melissa Etheridge sort of voice. Sexy.

And she *is* sexy—with her purple

31

mohawk and her gauged ears and her '80s-era Madonna fashion sense.

But we tried dating back in college, and when we fell onto the couch in Azure's dorm and started making out for the first time, we both laughed—hysterically—for a full fifteen minutes. The kissing itself wasn't laughable. Azure is passionate about everything she does, and she kissed me like she meant it. But it just felt...funny. Weird. Like we were kissing our sisters. So we made a pact then and there that we worked best as friends. And over time, we became *best* friends. And, eventually, co-workers.

I hurry out into the wet, humid air, the shop bells jangling behind me as the door creaks shut. There was a thunderous downpour a couple of hours ago, and the gray sky is still sprinkling. "Mia?" I say, holding the phone to my ear. I cross the street, splashing through puddles, and aim toward my junk heap of a car. Then I swing the door open—I never bother locking it; any car thief would be doing me a *big* favor—and fold myself onto the ripped, camel-colored seat with a sigh. "Sorry about that, baby. What's up?"

"Oh, God, you're never going to believe this, Court! You know that activist I was telling you about the other day? Drew Yarrow? She's the one who—"

"Yeah, I know who she is." I lean back

against the headrest and close my eyes for a moment, exhaling through my nose. My damp hair is sticking to my forehead, and there are wet strands clinging to my white button-down shirt. I shove my hair behind my shoulders as I stare, unseeing, at the water droplets gleaming on the windshield. "Drew Yarrow got arrested for staging that violent protest outside the Cincy Safe Center. It was all over the news. And I told you, Mia, that I don't think that's something you should involve yourself with, not for the sake of a story. It's dangerous and—"

"But I had lunch with her today, Court, and she told me what happened, what *really* happened. The networks got it all wrong. The rally was supposed to be peaceful. It only got violent because some vamps came out of the Center and went after Drew's group. One of her guys got *bit*—"

"Mia!" In lieu of gaping at Mia herself, I gape at my cell phone. "You're a newspaper reporter. *Consider the source*. Besides, that woman was convicted of *hate crimes*—"

"The charges were dropped. She was totally set up. There's so much corruption involved in this, baby. Oh, my God, the stories she told me..."

I cradle my forehead; my temples are throbbing to the rhythm of the rain, which has begun to fall hard again, pattering on the car's roof. "Of course Drew's going to tell you that she wasn't to blame—"

"It's *true*, Courtney. I can read people, you know. That's what makes me a good reporter. I know when someone's being straight with me, and Drew Yarrow is as straight as they come." She pauses, then laughs. "Well, she's not *straight* straight. Just honest. You know what I mean."

"Yeah, Mia," I mutter, staring at the rain streaking down my windshield. "I know what you mean."

Mia and I have been dating for five months, and when you've known someone for five months, you begin to notice patterns of behavior. Little things, like the fact that Mia always craves ice cream after sex, and big things, like the fact that Mia develops hero-worship crushes on women she finds fascinating. She's assured me that she'd never *act* on any of her crushes, but once upon a time, *I* was her crush. And she left her girlfriend of two years to begin a relationship with me.

So, Exhibit A: My girlfriend is infatuated with an anti-vampire radical—who (coincidentally enough) happens to be a lesbian.

Exhibit B: As of five minutes ago, *I* have a crush on a vampire.

I draw in a deep breath, but the bowling ball has become a boulder.

The ground beneath me feels shaky, tilted...

And I feel sick.

Sighing, I shove the key into the ignition with unnecessary ferocity. Then I gasp, disbelieving, because Colonel Mustard starts on the first try.

Well, at least something is going right today.

I switch my cell onto speakerphone and drop it into the empty cup holder.

"So, *any*way, I know we had plans to catch that new Tilda Swinton movie at the Cineplex tonight—" mutters Mia, like she's rehearsed the line.

I pull out onto the road.

"—but Drew's anti-vampire group—they're called SANG—is having their weekly meeting at seven, and I just kind of wanted to check it out, you know, because there might be a killer story there. Vampire journalism is so hot right now, and, I mean, a well-known leader of the AV movement? What a catch! I haven't had a big article in months. Malcolm threatened to demote me to Obituaries if I don't pull a rabbit out of my hat soon."

I nurse the brake and come to a full stop as the streetlight turns red. Then I tap my nails on the steering wheel distractedly. I painted my nails blue for Mia—blue's her favorite color—but she didn't notice my cobalt lacquer during dinner at my place last night.

She didn't notice my blue nails when I

undressed her, slowly — blouse and silky skirt and panties (Mia never wears a bra) — or when I trailed my fingers over her naked body, sometimes stroking, sometimes scratching, because she likes it when I scratch...

Lately, it seems like she doesn't notice a lot of things.

But then again, neither do I. After all, I forgot about our movie date. *Azure* remembered, and I didn't. That's got to be a bad sign...

"Courtney? *Hello?*"

"I'm here." The light turns green, and — predictably — Colonel Mustard stalls. I swear under my breath, ignoring the honking horns as I pull out my key and stab it in again, praying to any deity who's listening to either help my car start or strike it dead with a bolt of lightning.

Frankly, I'd prefer the bolt of lightning.

"What do you say? Can I give you a rain check on the movie?" Mia's voice takes on that low, sultry tone that always turns my misgivings to mush. "I promise I'll make it up to you." She laughs suggestively. "With interest."

The car engine revs, and I sigh with relief, easing across the intersection and then making a left turn.

"Courtney?"

"It's all right, baby," I tell Mia, because I *was* looking forward to my bath and my book and my glasses of wine. *Definitely* a bad sign, choosing strawberry-scented bubbles and a reread of *Jane Eyre* over a night of Tilda Swinton-inspired sex with my girlfriend... But I'm too worn out to consider those ramifications right now.

"Are you sure? You aren't disappointed?"

I peer through my streaming windshield. The sky is fully dark now, thick with storm clouds. "No, no. I'm tired, anyway. I got a damaged shipment from UPS this morning. It was a major headache to straighten out. And I think I permanently offended one of our regular suppliers. So I'd prefer a quiet night in. Tilda can wait."

"Well, if you're sure..." Mia's using her soft, placating voice now, the voice she uses when she knows she's getting away with something and feels a little guilty—but not guilty enough to change her mind. "Hey, how about I treat you to dinner tomorrow night, before the movie?"

"Tomorrow?" I get a green light at the next intersection and turn onto my road. "Okay. That sounds great, baby."

"Pick you up at eight?"

"Mm. See you then. And..." I frown, remembering the SANG brochure that I shredded less than a half hour ago. Its message was so dark, fueled by narrow-mindedness, hatred and intolerance. Despite the fact that we have a vampire President, the United States is deeply divided over the "vampire agenda," as the right-wing pundits call it. There are a lot of AV groups—anti-vampire groups—like SANG calling for the President's impeachment and strict laws prohibiting vampire rights, and it seems like another one appears every week, making news with headline-grabbing protests and rallies.

Mia and I have never talked much about vampires, but I guess I always assumed that she shared my sentiments: they have as much right to a peaceful existence as any of us do. Vampires are *born* vampires. Geneticists are still working out the science behind vampire DNA, but it's an irrefutable fact that vampires require the ingestion of blood to survive. Plus, Bram Stoker and Anne Rice got it wrong. No one can *become* a vampire by being bitten by a vampire. You're either born one, or you aren't. There's no choice in the matter. It's biological.

And, as a lesbian, I know what it feels like to be discriminated against, to be judged and despised for something beyond my control. Every day I face the prospect of coming out, of being rejected for who I am. And Mia knows that pain, too. Acutely. Her parents disowned her when she came out of the closet at seventeen, and she spent a year on the streets, homeless and alone. The only family member who stuck by her side was her brother, who lost his life tragically, in a heartbreaking case of wrong-place-at-the-wrong-time.

So how could she defend a group that spews hatred about a minority?

Two words, Courtney: Drew Yarrow.

My frown deepens when my memory conjures up the still of Drew that I'd seen on the news. She kind of looked...like me. Tall and blonde, but her hair was cut short, and her expression was hard, with small, narrowed eyes. Pretty—and predatory.

I disagree with her cause, and I don't trust her with my girlfriend.

"Well." I squint at the road, trying to think of something pleasant to say. "I hope you get a good story tonight," I force out, feeling uneasy. "Just...be careful."

"Love you, Court."

"Yeah. I... I love you, too, baby."

Mia hangs up first. I toss my cell onto the passenger seat and then turn into my driveway, shutting Colonel Mustard off with a sigh.

Chapter Two: Dancing in the Dark

There's nothing in my mailbox besides another SANG brochure—they must have financial backers, because their marketing campaign is topnotch—the latest *Cincinnati Times* and my overdue electricity bill. I throw the mail and my phone onto the kitchen table, along with my car keys, and then scoop a purring Colette up from the floor. At six years old, Colette is still the size of a kitten. The vet says she's fine, just naturally small, and she compensates for her littleness with a big personality. And a big appetite.

I nuzzle her brown tabby head, and she licks the tip of my nose.

"It's just you and me tonight, Cole."

Still purring, she climbs onto my shoulder and meows in my ear. It's a familiar and piercing meow. Translation: *Enough cuddling! I'm starved!* She emphasizes the point by sinking her tiny claws into my neck, kneading until she draws pinpricks of blood. I've never heard of a feline vampire, but I have to admit—sometimes I wonder about Colette. She is, after all, supernaturally cute.

"All right, all right, I get it..."

I feed Colette and then grab a Tupperware container from the refrigerator. I made vegetable lasagna for Mia last night, and there are plenty of leftovers. Colette crunches on kibble contentedly at my feet as I reach for a knife.

And then the world goes black.

I'm so startled by the sudden darkness that I drop the knife and scream, terrified that the blade might fall on my cat, but it connects with my wrist, instead, gashing the skin before clattering into the stainless steel sink basin. The lasagna follows behind, making a sickening plop.

"Oh, God..."

Great. A power outage. And if the searing pain is any indication, this cut is deep. I press my palm against it and feel hot blood seeping from the wound. A *lot* of blood. I fumble with the hot water knob and wash the blood from my hand; then I stand in the middle of the kitchen uselessly, clasping my wrist from underneath. The first-aid kit is in the bathroom upstairs, but given the power outage and the black-as-night, stormy sky, I can't see my hand in front of my face...

Maybe the lights will come back on soon. Power outages don't usually last long in my neighborhood. I mean, if this even *is* a power outage. What if the electric company shut off my power because I'm two months behind on payments? God, that would be such a spectacularly crappy ending to my already crappy day...

I peel back the curtain over the sink; the whole street is dark. Relieved, I lick my lips, and my shoulders relax. But then I lean closer to the glass.

There's a ball of light in the yard of the vacant house next door, and it's bouncing closer—

"Hello?" A woman's voice, heard clearly through my open window.

I drop the curtain and take a step back.

"Hello? Are you all right?"

Is she talking to me? Cautiously, I draw the curtain again, but the light is gone, and it's too dark to make out any shapes beyond the window.

I squint into the blackness.

And someone knocks at the kitchen door.

"Who—who's there?" I stammer, leaning back against the sink. Colette is still at my feet, unbothered and nibbling away; I nearly trip over her as I move in the general direction of the door. To prevent myself from hurting her, I perform the time-honored cat-trip ballet and throw my weight forward, colliding with the refrigerator and nicking my temple. *"Oof,"* I mutter. *Smooth, Court. Real smooth.*

"Hello?" the voice calls out again. An oddly familiar, low voice. "I heard a scream when the lights went out. Are you hurt?"

"Um..." I reach the door and place my hand on the knob, but I don't unlock it. There's actually something *very* familiar about this woman's voice. I can't place her, though. Of course, I don't know everyone on the street. I've lived here for three years, as long as I've been in charge of the bookstore, but I spend so much time working that I rarely see my neighbors in the daylight. Besides, as a single lesbian living alone, I carefully consider the people I take into my confidence. Colette is a fierce little feline, but she isn't exactly a guard dog.

Right now, though, given the fact that I'm bleeding and stumbling blind in the dark, maybe I should throw caution to the wind and accept this offer of help. Mia's always saying I need to be more spontaneous. I'm just not sure if inviting a stranger into my home is *spontaneous* so much as *reckless*...

But what the hell.

I unlock the door and open it just a crack. "Hi—oh! Hi." My lips part, and for a moment, I think I must be hallucinating. Maybe I've lost more blood than I realized...

Because standing on my back deck with a glowing camping lantern in one hand is Valeria Máille. Lare, the alchemy-inclined vampire.

The *sexy*, alchemy-inclined vampire. Her sugared lily scent wafts toward me, and I start to feel even more lightheaded.

I start to feel...*other* things, too.

But—wait. Did she follow me here? *Oh, God, Courtney, don't be a bigot.* She left the store before I did, so it's unlikely that she *stalked* me to my house. This isn't *Interview with the Vampire*. This is real life. In real life, there are power outages. In real life, friendly neighbors offer assistance.

But Lare isn't my neighbor. Is she? This part of town is Code A, Free Residence, meaning vampires are permitted to move in without neighborhood petition, but I wasn't aware of any vampires living nearby. And I really think I would have been aware of *Lare* living nearby.

"Um, hi," I say again, flustered. Then I blink and shake my head, smiling nervously. "What are you—how did you—I mean, do you live around here? I've never—"

"You're bleeding," Lare says, and her eyes, lit up by the lantern, widen and gleam. They're so reflective that I can see myself in them; I look crazed, scared. I guess I am scared. But kind of...excited-scared. Roller-coaster scared. Cake-for-dinner scared. You know it's bad for you—but you want it, anyway.

You want it a *lot*.

Mia, Courtney. Remember Mia...

Mia—who's probably making puppy dog eyes at Drew Yarrow right now.

Sighing, I push my hair behind my shoulders and bite my lip. Logically speaking, I should be plain old *scared*-scared, because it's dark, and there's a vampire at my door, and she's staring, mesmerized, at my bloody arm.

Reflexively, I cover the wound with my hand. "I don't think the cut's serious—"

"You might need stitches. Can I take a look?"

"Um."

What's the proper etiquette for this situation? On the one hand, I don't want to offend a potential customer. On the *other* hand, I'm not sure if presenting my bleeding appendage to a vampire is a wise move.

Lare shifts the lantern lower, and her eyes lose their mirror-like quality. Now they're shining pools of deep, dark blue. I gaze into them, fall into them...

And then I hear myself say, "Sure, why not?"

Sure, why not?

My blood runs cold. I freeze in place, eyes as wide as saucers.

Lare's mouth curves up on one side, and she leans against the door frame; her face is inches away from mine. Her red waves are caught in a gust, and they brush against my face, soft as silk—and a little damp... "Mind if I come in, then?" she asks, voice low.

"I—"

"Because I'm getting pretty wet out here."

It's only then that I realize that Lare is

standing in the rain. Her white shirt is soaked through—she's no longer wearing the pinstripe jacket—and tiny droplets of water cling to her lashes. As if on cue, there's a crack of thunder overhead, followed by an eye-burning streak of lightning, illuminating my darkened yard and backlighting Lare like a sexy, dripping, rock 'n' roll star.

"Sorry. God, I'm sorry. Come on in. I'll find you a towel."

She chuckles. "Thanks."

By the time Lare has dried her hair and scrubbed some of the dampness from her clothing—I'm trying hard not to stare at her shirt (honestly, I *am*), but it's wet and it's *white*, clinging to her lace-patterned bra—my wrist begins to throb. I fall into one of the chairs, resting my arm on the kitchen table's cluttered surface. Colette curls up into a tabby-striped ball at my feet.

Lare places her lantern in the center of the table, and when she sits down across from me, I realize, horrified, that the SANG brochure is brightly spotlighted by the lantern's white bulb.

Her eyes flick toward it, pause, and then lift, with meaningful slowness, to meet my gaze.

I feel the color drain from my face. "I don't—I'm not—"

"Junk mail. I know. I got one of these, too." She picks up the brochure and examines it, smiling faintly. "SANG: Society for the

Abolishment of Nocturnal Ghouls," she reads, one eyebrow raised. Then she smiles softly. "Funny thing is...vampires aren't really nocturnal. We just don't sleep as often as you."

"Me?"

"Humans."

"I'm...sorry. I was going to throw it away, but then the lights went out—"

"You don't have to apologize for other people's ignorance, Courtney." Her silver-blue eyes bore through me; I feel hot and cold all at once.

"It's just... Well, to be honest, I don't know a lot about vampires myself. I feel like I keep, well, offending you, and that's the last thing I want to do—"

"You haven't offended me." Lare leans forward and reaches across the table, stroking my open palm lightly with her charcoal-polished nail. I flutter my eyelids as a delicious shiver moves through my body; for a moment, I forget about my cut, about Mia and Drew, about my broken-down car and the flimsy financial state of the bookstore. I forget about everything, feeling nothing but this sensation, this...longing—

"Courtney." Lare's voice is soft, husky. I shiver again, staring into her color-shifting eyes.

"Yeah?"

She draws back her hand. "Do you have a first-aid kit?"

I swallow, will my hammering heart to

slow, and then nod my head. "Upstairs."

I give Lare directions to the bathroom; she takes her lantern and returns a few minutes later with a damp paper towel, antibiotic cream and bandages. Then, like a knight in a Pre-Raphaelite painting, she kneels in her soaking clothes in front of my chair and reaches for my hand. Her eyes catch mine; they're glinting impishly. "Don't worry. I'm a doctor."

I laugh—nervously, too loudly.

"No, really." Her warm fingers stroke the delicate skin of my wrist, just above the wound. "I'm not practicing right now, though. I'm doing some research at GLT."

"GLT?" I'd noticed the acronym on the business card she gave me at the store.

"Give Life Technologies—the big gray building over on Truman Avenue."

"Oh, right." That's the building everyone calls Blood Mart; it's where the packets for the local Safe Center are produced. I didn't realize it was a research facility as well as a production plant. "What sort of research do you do?"

She smiles. "Well, right now my work is at a standstill. Which is why I'm eager to read any writings by or about Maximinus that you're able to track down." Gently, Lare moves her hands to the underside of my arm and lowers her face nearer to my wound. To *look* at it, I'm sure. Not to *lick* it. Not to *bite* it...

"Um." My mouth has gone as dry as

49

sandpaper, and I feel two breaths away from fight-or-flight panic. "I appreciate your help — it was really nice of you to check up on me — but I'm just kind of... Well, you're a... You're a vampire. And I'm bleeding. And — I don't mean to — oh, God, sorry. I'm just...clueless about all of this." I rake my free hand back through my hair, which is so tangled that my fingers get caught up in knots; with the grace of a grizzly bear on stilts, I yank my fingers free — nearly knocking the lantern over in the process. I right the tilting lantern and then sink down in my chair, humiliated.

Despite my *faux pas,* a smile teases the corners of Lare's lips. "I promise you: I didn't come here to" — her eyes trail over my throat — "bite your neck," she finishes, in an exaggerated Dracula-style accent. She chuckles lightly.

"I know. I mean, logically, I know that." After all, if she'd wanted to, as she put it, *bite my neck*, she could've done so right away, when I let her into the house. "It's just..." My smile is uncertain. "Okay, I have to ask..." I give her a pleading look. "Did you follow me? I mean, it's...strange, your showing up at my door tonight. Coincidental. We met at the bookstore today, and then — "

"I just moved into the house next door." Lare tilts her head of red waves, gesturing vaguely toward the window and the brick one-story that had been vacant since last winter. "I'd been renting an apartment on the west side, but my contract with GLT was extended, so I wanted a more permanent residence." She smiles at me softly. "I'm sorry, Courtney. I thought you realized I'd moved in. I shouldn't have assumed. But didn't you see the U-Haul yesterday? It was parked next to your driveway."

Yesterday. I bite my lip. Yesterday I came home from work, made dinner for Mia, had sex with Mia...and then slept the deep, dreamless sleep of the stressed and exhausted. "I guess I was distracted." Another thing I'd failed to notice, or remember. When did I start sleepwalking through life?

"I admit—it still seems coincidental." Lare begins to wash off my cut with the wet paper towel, her silver-blue eyes affixed to her task. Then she pauses, looks up—and she gazes at me so deeply that my heart loses track of time, forgets to beat. Her teasing mouth slants to one side. "But I don't believe in coincidences."

I swallow. "Don't you?"

Lare shakes her head as she leans close to my arm, peering at the gash in the meager light of the lantern. "Ah, good news. You won't need stitches, after all."

"That's great," I say softly. I watch her; I can hardly *breathe*, watching her. I'm not like this. I don't swoon. I don't contemplate *cheating*. I don't fantasize about kissing vampires. I do what I'm supposed to do. I was a Girl Scout. I was an honor student. Despite my sugar addiction, I've never even had a cavity.

But suddenly—staring at the fine red strands grazing Lare's neck; at her lips, faintly pink, concealing those sharp white teeth—what I'm supposed to do isn't so obvious.

I think my intuition, like the electricity, has winked out.

"Tell me if this hurts," Lare says, but she's so gentle, I hardly feel the pressure of her fingers at all as she treats and bandages my arm with slow, steady motions. Her palms are so warm. "You'll be sore for a couple of days, but I don't think the skin will scar."

"Oh. That's..." I swallow. "Thank you. And...sorry. I feel stupid for screaming. I hope I didn't startle you."

"I'm not easily startled." She smiles up at me, her fingers still resting on my arm, adjusting the gauze. "Besides, mankind's first and deepest fear is of the dark." Lare's mirrored eyes reflect the lantern light, the rose-patterned wall behind me, my mesmerized face. "You were acting on instinct. Instinct won't lead you astray."

Given the fact that my *instinct* is telling me to straddle Lare on the floor...I'm not sure that I can agree with her sentiment. I swallow again, glancing down at Colette, who's still dreaming beside my feet. "This is Colette, by the way. She'll never forgive me if I don't introduce her properly. She's a bit of a snob."

"Colette?" She smiles. "You named your cat after the French novelist?"

"I went through a francophile phase in grad school."

Lare rises from the floor and offers me her hand. I take it gingerly—touching her makes me feel too hot, too shaky, too impulsive—and stand up. "Colette's a perfect name for a cat," she says. "Colette loved cats, as I recall. How does the line go? *Time spent with a cat is never wasted.*"

"She also said, *There are no ordinary cats.* And my Colette is extraordinary." I give the sleepy tabby an affectionate nudge with my toes, and she begins to purr. "I volunteered at an animal shelter for a while." I smile at Lare self-deprecatingly. "I'd like to pretend it was for some noble reason, but I had a crush on the woman who ran the place."

Lare lifts a brow, amused. Standing so close to her is making me feel dizzy. "And how did that work out for you?" she asks, voice low.

"Oh, I didn't get the girl—she was straight, and engaged—but I got Colette." I laugh. "I was never a cat person, you know. Or a dog person. But one look into those beautiful green eyes, and my heart kind of melted."

"I know the feeling." Lare pins me down with her intense, silver gaze. She shoves her hands into her pockets and tilts her head; red

53

waves tumble over her shoulder. She smiles. "That's what I was talking about—instinct. Sometimes you just...know."

"Yeah." I draw in a shallow breath. "Sometimes you do. Even though..." I trail off.

"Even though what, Courtney?"

I narrow my brows, staring down at the terra cotta-colored floor tiles. "Even though, rationally speaking," I find myself rambling miserably, "you *shouldn't* do what your instinct is telling you to do. Because it would change everything. It would unravel your whole life. It would compromise your beliefs about yourself, about the world—"

"Hey." Lare takes a small step closer. "Are we still talking about cats?"

"No." I meet her eyes brazenly, stare at her mouth brazenly. There's no power in the house right now, but electricity crackles between us: a tense, dangerous, vital thing. "How do you do it?" I ask Lare then, surprising myself.

"Do...what?" She arches one brow, biting her bottom lip so that her right incisor stabs, softly, into the soft pink flesh there. I can't tear my eyes away from that tooth, can't wrap my mind around the fact that Lare is a *vampire*, a real-life vampire. She's different from me, genetically different. She drinks blood to survive. She'll live for more than a century. Vampires aren't immortal, but they age at a slower rate and enjoy three times the lifespan of human beings. Maybe she's already lived for hundreds of years.

"How do you control yourself?" I whisper.

She blinks, uncomprehending. Then her silver eyes trace over my mouth.

I shiver. She isn't touching me, but I *feel* her touching every part of me. Is this a vampire thing? Or am I just—suddenly, deeply, uncontrollably—*smitten*? "I mean," I say, pulse racing, "with the blood."

Her posture straightens. Slowly, she draws her hands out of her pants pockets and crosses her arms over her chest. "I'm not sure what you're asking."

"I only want to understand. You... You said you're a doctor. Doctors have to deal with other people's blood. And just now, with my arm—was it hard for you? I mean, is it hard to be around humans?" I swallow, gazing at her uncertainly. My skin is on fire, every atom aching and aware. "Is it hard to be around me?"

"Yes," she answers quickly, simply. Her face is still and smooth, unreadable. But then I see her shoulders relax, and a smile teases at the corner of her lovely mouth. "But not for the reason you're suggesting."

My heart triple-beats.

I gaze at Lare in the light of the lantern, at her silver eyes and her long, curving silhouette. She looks like an art nouveau painting. There's a flowing, liquid grace to her body, her gestures. And a hungry, fearless gleam to her eyes.

Tiger-like, I think. I'll have to tell Azure. In the Banks' Books customer zoo, Lare is the tiger.

And now Lare, the tiger, the vampire, prowls nearer to me.

I hold my breath, tilting my mouth toward hers.

"Courtney," she breathes, "do you feel—"

Then, with rude and blinding brightness, the lights flick back on.

Frowning, exhaling, I glare up at the ceiling fixture. The room looks harsh now, too clear. Too real. And Lare has moved away, glanced away. She's shoved her hands into her pockets again, and she's staring at the door; she's planning to leave.

Nothing's going to happen between us tonight.

I don't know whether I'm disappointed or relieved.

No, that's a lie. I'm disappointed—and disappointed in myself for *being* disappointed.

God, I'm so confused.

Absurdly, my empty stomach chooses that moment to—very audibly—growl.

"Well." Lare chuckles, nodding in the direction of my complaining belly. "I'll leave you to your dinner. I was about to, um, *eat*, too, so..."

I start to suggest to her that we dine together, but then I realize what Lare meant by *eat*—and decide that we might feel a bit awkward sharing a meal: me with my cold, sink-battered lasagna, Lare with her cold packet of blood.

"Van Helsing's probably trying to break down my door, anyway," she says.

"What?" Lost in my own thoughts, I shake my head. I must have misheard her. "Did you say Van Helsing?"

"Yeah."

My brain feels untethered, floaty, unable to distinguish between fact and fairy tale. But what the hell do I know? Vampires exist. Maybe vampire hunters exist, too. "Van Helsing is a fictional character, though...right?"

She laughs, her blue eyes twinkling with silver flashes, like stars fading in and out. "Of course. Fictional. Like Dracula and Carmilla and Lestat. And Edward Cullen." Her lovely smile widens. "But Helly is also a very real, very slobbery Saint Bernard. And I haven't let him out since this morning, so he has every right to be cross with me."

"Oh—you have a Saint Bernard?"

"Well... I think a more accurate statement would be that Van Helsing has *me*, but... Yeah. He's my faithful—and only—companion. We've been together for a long time, Helly and I."

I wonder what constitutes a "long time"

to a vampire. Fifty years? Eighty? Two hundred? But dogs don't live that long, obviously. At least, as far as I know. I'm beginning to realize how very little I *do* know.

Lare opens the kitchen door, glancing back at me over her shoulder as she steps halfway outside. The scent of ozone and wet grass wafts through the wide, dark opening. "Look after that cut. If it gets infected, let me know, and I'll take care of you."

I'll take care of you. I nod and smile, despite my jackhammering heart, and lift my hand in a finger-curling wave. "Thank you again. I mean...I don't know *how* to thank you. If you hadn't come, I would've probably knocked myself out trying to climb upstairs in the dark."

"It was my pleasure." She grins—a slow, teasing grin that makes my knees weak and my heart a dumb, useless muscle in my chest. From a logical standpoint, I realize that those pointy vampire fangs are—*literally*—designed to kill mortals like me... But, *God*, does she look sexy when she smiles. Maybe that's part of the allure Azure was talking about earlier today. Maybe I'm *supposed* to be attracted to every dangerous aspect of this woman; maybe I'm supposed to desire her, to feel compelled to be near her, like some hapless prey animal.

Or maybe I've just watched one too many lesbian vampire movies.

Either way, an object in motion will stay

in motion... I take a deep breath and return her smile. "I'd... I'd love to repay the favor sometime. I mean, not that I want you to slice your arm open in a similar feat of epic clumsiness or anything, but—" I flush, tongue-tied. I feel like I'm back in high school, trying to catch the interest of Marly Blackwater, the gorgeous head cheerleader—and failing miserably. I had then, as I still have now, a terminal case of I-don't-know-what-to-say-itis. The only reason Mia and I ever hooked up at all was because she was the aggressor—and because Mia Foster always gets what she wants.

"Like I said, I was happy to help." Lare tilts her head at me, offering another electric grin. "No repayment necessary. Just let me know if you unearth anything about Maximinus, okay?" she says, and she begins to close the door behind her.

"Sure." I smile weakly. "Um, see you around?"

"*Au revoir.*" She shuts the door with a click.

I glance down, bleakly, at the flickering orange-yellow flame: Lare left her lantern burning on my kitchen table. I flick it off with a sigh and then walk to the sink to salvage the remains of the lasagna. It lies floppy and disordered in the bottom of the sink, a confusion of limp pasta and faded vegetables—and, really, it's an apt (and unappetizing) visual metaphor for my current mental state.

Looking at the lasagna makes me think of Mia, and I don't want to think of Mia. Not right now, not tonight. I don't want to think about what she's doing, who she's with. I don't want to think about the fact that I would rather spend my night alone than with my girlfriend.

Alone...or accompanied by the vampire next door.

My heart pounds harder in my chest at the mere thought of Lare.

Stop it, Courtney. This isn't some paranormal soap opera. This is your life. Be sensible.

As I scoop the lasagna corpse out of the sink, I resolve to pass the evening doing exactly what I told Azure I would do, given the choice: I'll draw a bath, and I'll read *Jane Eyre*, and I'll get really, really warm and soft and philosophical and slightly—or maybe very, *very*—drunk.

But first...

My stomach growls again—this time, angrily.

I shuffle over to the table, grab my cell phone, and order a pizza, extra cheese.

Chapter Three: All the Wrong Decisions

I'm booting up the store laptop when Azure tosses a stack of bills and the latest copy of the *Times* onto the desk. "That shipment from Aurora is late, and you got a call from some guy in Kentucky who claims he has a first edition of *Moll Flanders*." She frowns, shoving a stray purple spike back into place. "But he sounded weird. Whacked. I don't know if it's the real deal or not. Here's his number, in case you want to call back. Personally, I wouldn't advise it." She hands me a white slip of paper; then she raises one eyebrow and gives me a wry look. "So how'd the tryst go last night?"

I choke on my coffee, nearly dropping my beloved *I Read Banned Books* mug. "Tr—tryst?"

"With Jane. Jane *Eyre*. You know, that sassy little governess. Don't tell me she stood you up?"

I sit down, placing my coffee cup on top of the newspaper on the desk, and offer Azure a small smile. "No, Jane was great. Jane's always great." Except I couldn't focus on my reading, so I spent the entire length of my bubble bath fantasizing about Lare—and hating myself for it. I take another sip of my too-hot coffee: I deserve a burned tongue. "How was *your* night, Az?"

"Dull. I wrote some lyrics and then zombied out in front of *Friends* on the sofa. I don't even like *Friends*. God, being an adult sucks." She sulks for a split-second, then brightens. "But you know what *doesn't* suck?"

"What?" I laugh.

"*This*." She grabs the *Times*, nearly spilling my coffee, and points to a headline on the front page:

Local Music Fest Allies with Cincy Safe Center

I take the paper from her and quickly skim the article.

"Isn't it awesome, Court? A portion of the ticket proceeds are going to go toward community vampire education. Scott—he's the head organizer of the music fest—is a vampire, so it's a cause close to his heart, obviously. Plus—listen to this!" She waves her hands excitedly. "He just signed that all-vamp group Triple Helix to headline the festival." Azure jumps up and down. "I can't believe I'm going to perform on the same stage as Triple Helix! I feel like a *real* rock star now."

"You *are* a real rock star," I tell her, putting down the paper and digging my cell phone out of my purse. "I can't wait to see you shine on the stage—*finally*." I smile. "I'm so proud of you, Az."

She squeezes me in a tight hug. "Man, I have *way* too much energy this morning. Sorry if I talk your ear off or start running up and down the aisles. I'm just so stoked!"

I laugh, squeezing her back. Then she lets go and takes off to finish sorting the morning's deliveries, singing quietly as she works. I listen to her sing as I draw in a deep breath, staring at the phone in my hand.

Then I dial Mia's number.

No answer.

She's at the office, probably working. No reason to be concerned.

I call again during my lunch break. Still no answer—and my overactive imagination begins, well, actively imagining Drew Yarrow, the anti-vampire revolutionary, feeding chocolate-dipped strawberries to my besotted girlfriend...

Cool it, Courtney. You're jumping to conclusions. And being kind of a hypocrite.

Besides, Mia hates strawberries, and she's lactose intolerant, so she can't even digest most brands of chocolate —

I drop a heavy box of books on my left foot and bite my tongue to prevent myself from yowling in pain, because Azure's waiting on a customer at the front of the store. I only whimper—more from the pain of biting my tongue than from the fifty pounds of books crushing my toes. I can taste blood in my mouth, which makes me think of Lare, which makes me feel guilty, which makes me think of Mia, which makes me feel confused...

I pick up the box again and carry it behind the desk, taking care not to upset the bandage on my arm. Turns out the cut wasn't as deep as it felt; I put fresh gauze on it this morning and was kind of disappointed to realize I wouldn't need to take Lare up on her offer for more medical assistance...

Well, there's no better cure for mental chaos than tedious organization, so I throw myself into the task of adding our latest literary acquisitions to the computer inventory. Entering the titles, authors, ISBNs, publication dates, and condition descriptions soothes my overstimulated mind. I work for hours, and when I finish and glance up from the desk, Azure's sweeping the floor with the broom—and giving me an accusatory, knowing stare.

"You're upset about something," she says, pausing in her task to put her hand—still clutching the dustpan—on her hip while shaking her purple head. "What's going on, Courtney?"

"Nothing's going on." I smile—or try to smile, but Azure always knows when I'm faking it, and I'm really, really faking it right now.

She points the bristles of the broom at me menacingly, narrowing her dark green eyes. "Come on, boss. Spill. Don't make me tickle it out of you."

I laugh. "Oh, God, no tickling, please." In college, Azure accidentally discovered my Achilles heel: I can't bear being tickled, and, as irony would have it, I'm *intensely* ticklish. So my well-meaning but wicked best friend has blackmailed me with this knowledge on more than one occasion. The last time she pulled the "Do this or I'll tickle you" card, she was trying to convince me to go out on a date with a girl—Margie—she had met at a club during one of her performances. "She's totally your type," Azure had promised me, but Margie, although a book lover, spent our entire night out complaining about the food (it was bland and too cold), the weather (it was damp and ruining her hair), the movie (it was boring and derivative). She probably complained about our quick good-night kiss to her roommate afterward—and she would have had a right to complain about it. It *was* chaste and indifferent. Needless to say, we never went out again.

Azure sighs, putting down her broom of doom and regarding me with softened, sympathetic eyes. "Is this about Mia and that woman from the museum?"

"No, no, she got over her," I say dismissively, waving a hand in the air. Mia had had a crush on the curator at the arts museum—or a "deep admiration," as she called it. But the curator made some offhand, homophobic remarks, so Mia promptly lost interest in Monet and Cassat. "And she swears nothing happened between them."

"Then is it the woman who works at the book arts place?

"No. Straight. Married."

"How about the roller derby girl?"

I frown. "Mia *did* kiss her, but that was ages ago. And Mia confessed, apologized... She said she was drunk when it happened—"

"Court...she's taking advantage of you."

I fall into the chair behind the desk and close my eyes. "She's just... She can't help it. That's who she is. She's never actually *cheated*. And I know she loves me, Azure—"

"That isn't the point," she huffs. "That isn't romance. And a kiss *is* cheating. Hold on a second." She runs down one of the aisles, and I hear her drag a step-stool up to a shelf and pull one of the books out, swearing quietly beneath her breath as the stool makes a wobbly sound. She returns a moment later with a broad, triumphant smile.

"This," she says dramatically, brandishing the red, cloth-bound copy of *Jane Eyre*, "is *romance*." She flips through the book, then flips some more. "Give me a second. I haven't read this novel since freshman year. Ah! Here we go..." She clears her throat.

"'I sometimes have a *queer* feeling with regard to you,'" Azure reads, emphasizing the word *queer*, with a knowing grin, "'especially when you are near me, as now: it is as if I had a string somewhere under my left ribs, tightly and inextricably knotted to a similar string situated in the corresponding quarter of your little frame. And if that boisterous channel and two hundred miles or so of land come broad between us, I am afraid that cord of communion will be snapped; and then I've a nervous notion I should take to bleeding inwardly.'

"Now," Azure says, in a mock British accent, snapping the book closed, "tell me, Courtney Banks—have you ever experienced that sort of connection with Mia Foster?"

I pretend to consider. But, honestly, there's nothing *to* consider. Mia and I fit together in some important ways: we're attracted to each other; we respect one another's dreams and professions; we both have serious infatuations with the written word.

But there is a disconnect.

There is a...lack. A lack that provokes Mia to crush on other women, and me to ignore my misgivings by burying myself in work and living vicariously through escapist fiction. A lack that prevents us from fully committing and moving in together.

A lack that we both feel but—purposefully, carefully—never, *ever* talk about.

"Well, *have* you?" Azure presses.

"No," I answer; then I stand up and take

the book from her hands. "But how many people *ever* find a love like this? Is it even possible? I mean..." I gaze at the copy of *Jane Eyre* that Azure's holding dubiously. "Jane and Rochester don't exist. They never had to deal with electric bills or power outages or vampires moving in next door—"

"Vampires—wait. *What?*"

"Never mind," I say quickly, trading the book for the broom. I begin to sweep the already-swept floor with quick, nervous motions. "Anyway, I'm sure this thing with Drew Yarrow will pass. Mia will lose interest, just like she did with all of the others—"

"Drew Yarrow?" Azure, who had been absentmindedly bending a paperclip into a heart shape, freezes in place. "Drew *Yarrow*? The woman who launched the attack against the Safe Center that was all over the news?"

I nod, gazing up at Azure grimly. "The one and only."

"But she's—that's—I mean..." She squeezes the paperclip in her fist, then opens her fingers to reveal a mangled metal heart. "Courtney, Drew Yarrow's bad news. Have you read any of the articles about her online?"

I shake my head.

"Well, she's got some scary ideas about how to deal with the 'vampire plague,' as she calls it. We're talking *extermination*. I mean, it's messed up that Mia keeps chasing after other women when she's in an exclusive relationship with you—*really* messed up—but Drew Yarrow is a *supervillain*. And I didn't think Mia was part of the anti-vampire crowd. Is she?"

"I don't know, Azure." I drop the broom to check the store's email account on the laptop. Early in the morning (okay, first thing in the morning), I'd sent messages to my contacts with the details of Lare's Maximinus request.

Still no responses.

I slouch back to the chair and collapse onto it with an *oof.* "Can we change the subject?" I ask hopefully.

"I really think you should talk about this—"

"I know. I should. But...not right now, okay?"

Azure shakes her head. "You're being avoidant. That means this whole thing is really bugging you—"

"Thanks, Azure Freud," I smile teasingly, using the nickname some friends and I came up with for her in college. Azure minored in psychology, and she would have made an awesome psychologist; she's been my unpaid therapist for years. "You're right. It *is* bugging me, but..." I shift uncomfortably on the chair. "Something...*else* is kind of bugging me more."

She moves closer, pausing when she's standing beside me. "Something else?" Frowning, she narrows her eyes. "This sounds serious."

"It kind of is. And kind of isn't." I cradle my head in my hands. "Azure, I think I'm having a midlife crisis."

"Oh, Court." She rests a hand on my shoulder. "I'm sorry if I was a little harsh about Mia. I just care about you and—"

"I know, I know. The problem is..." I look up at her and chew on my bottom lip guiltily. "I think I almost—well, not almost—but I *might* have—but I don't know, really, because the lights came back on—but I really, really *wanted* to—"

"Hey." Azure holds up a hand, laughing lightly. "Can I get a complete sentence here? Your dangling phrases are making me dizzy."

"Sorry." I grimace, raking a hand back through my hair—which is marginally less tangled than it was yesterday evening. Should I do this? Should I confess to Azure? She isn't a priest, and I'm not Catholic. But my brain keeps running in circles, and it might calm down if I voice some of my shameful, guilt-ridden, befuddled thoughts aloud.

I take a deep breath. "So. I'm sort of in lust with a vampire."

For a moment, Azure only stares at me, arms and ankles crossed, leaning against the desk with a furrowed brow, her purple mohawk tilted to one side. She's so still that I begin to wonder whether time has stopped, or slowed, or ceased to exist—after all, if vampires are real, time travel can't be far behind—but the second hand on the wall clock is steadily ticking around. Finally, she straightens and offers me a confused stare. "Okay. I just needed a second to compute. So, what you're saying is...you're having an affair with a vampire?"

"No! No, I haven't had *anything* with a vampire—no affairs, no kisses."

"No interviews?" she asks wryly.

I smirk. "No interviews. Yet." I wring my hands in my lap. "And I don't intend to have any...interviews. But... Well, you met Lare. You know—"

"*Lare?*" Azure's eyes leap out of her head—or look as if they have, they're so wide. She loses her balance and has to catch herself by grabbing onto the desk, but her gaze—stunned and gleaming like green beach glass—never leaves my face. "You're having an affair with a *customer?*"

I fold my arms across my middle and shake my head, a little sulkily. "No, Az. I'm just attracted to her. Very attracted to her. Rochester-and-Jane attracted to her. And," I say, smiling weakly, "turns out she's my new next-door neighbor."

"*What?*"

"I don't know if it's fate or karma or coincidence, but I'm feeling, you know, *weird* about the whole thing. She came over last night and"—I roll up my shirt sleeve and show Azure my bandaged arm—"treated my knife wound."

"*Knife* wound?"

"Don't worry. It didn't happen in a dark alleyway."

"Then where—"

"A dark kitchen. The power went out, and I dropped the knife in a very clumsy way." I shrug then, pushing my sleeve back down. "And apparently Lare's a doctor."

Azure gives me a withering glance. "A vampire doctor. Seriously?"

"Seriously."

"Okay, you know I'm pro-vamp all the way. But that's... That's like inviting a cannibal to a dinner party. Or a recovering drug addict to a pot-smoking shindig. It isn't cool. It's a disservice to everyone involved. I mean, you can't really *blame* the cannibal for eating your Aunt Frida, because it *was* a dinner party, after all. He arrived hungry—"

"I know." I chew on my thumbnail. "I have to admit—I was worried about that, too. But Lare was calm and...business-like around my blood. She didn't seem to mind it, or crave it. And, Az, there was a *lot* of blood—"

"Still—"

"Maybe vampires have more self-control than we give them credit for." I lift a brow at Azure and bite my bottom lip, remembering Lare's gentle fingers on my skin, her steady gaze, silver and unblinking, reflecting my own anxious eyes...

"Courtney, what are you trying to tell me here?"

"I... I don't know." Distracted, I shake my head. "There's something about Lare that just..."

"Just what?"

I sigh, frustrated, and look up at Azure helplessly. "I've never been a love-at-first-sight kind of person. You know that."

She chuckles, sinking down onto the low footstool behind the desk, and begins to retie the trailing shoelaces of her lime green sneakers. "I remember you telling me in college—we were so drunk that night; it was after that party at Adele's—that you didn't believe in love, period. You said it was just a societal construct; a temporary, chemically induced brain dysfunction—"

"Did I really say that?" I ask quietly.

"As quoted." Azure nods, smiling a sad smile.

"God..." I stare at my hands in my lap. "I have no memory of ever saying that." Though I've *thought* it often enough. It's how I feel, how I've felt for my entire life—or at least since I was eight years old, when my parents, after a decade of screaming expletives at each other, finally split up.

Right now, Azure's revelation hits a little

too close to home. I've never told Mia that I'm *in* love with her, only that I love her. And I do love her. Despite her wandering eye, she's a phenomenal human being, so driven and *alive* and determined, and I feel honored to be a part of her life.

But the truth is...I'm not sure that I know what being *in* love feels like.

"All right." I swallow the lump in my throat. "So I'm a professed love skeptic."

"Love atheist, technically."

"Still, I've never cheated on anyone, not ever. So how could this happen? I mean, I don't think anything's *going* to happen between Lare and me, but I feel so guilty—"

"Listen." Azure stands up and then takes my hands, pulling me off of the chair until I'm standing, reluctantly, in front of her. She cups my chin and stares hard into my eyes. "The *reason* you don't believe in love is because you follow your head"—she taps my forehead—"you analytical Virgo, you, and not your *heart*." She taps the left side of my chest.

"Hey. No foreplay on the job."

"Sorry, boss." She grins, but then her expression becomes serious again. Bad sign. Azure is rarely serious. I swallow another lump in my throat and shift my gaze to the box of books on the floor. The novel on the top of the stack is, ironically enough, titled *So She Learned to Love*—a pulp fiction book from the sixties.

The cover depicts a blonde, Twiggy-esque woman looking perplexed as silhouetted couples embrace behind her.

"Now, if your heart is telling you to have a mad, reckless fling with a vampire doctor, *I* say go for it. Break things off with Mia. You haven't been happy in a long time, Court. And, I'd bet, neither has she."

"But..." My stomach sinks. "Are relationships actually about being happy?"

"*Yes!* Of course they are. Otherwise, what's the point?"

I gaze back at her uncomfortably. "Companionship? Orgasms? Someone to share takeout boxes with?"

Giving me a look that is somehow both stern and sympathetic at the same time, Azure reaches for the copy of *Jane Eyre* on the counter and presses it hard against my chest. "This is your bible. Study it. Memorize it. *Live* it."

"I can't..." I shake my head and smile. "I don't even know if I'm Rochester or Jane."

"Be either of them, both of them. Whatever! Just be happy, Court. Or else..." Azure poises her fingers menacingly, wiggling them in the universal gesture of *I'm going to tickle you*.

The door jangles open then, saving me from choosing between a panic-inducing promise or an equally panic-inducing ticklefest. With a last warning look, Azure turns around to go wait on the customer, and I return to the desk, distracting myself from my chemically induced brain dysfunction by picking up the newspaper and skimming the other articles.

I furrow my brows as I read the top story: *Give Life Technologies Scientist Missing, Presumed Kidnapped.*

My heart starts beating faster. Give Life Technologies is Lare's workplace. A quick scan of the article informs me that a chemist named Daniel Pascow went missing during the middle of his graveyard shift late last night. His co-workers searched the building for him; then they called his wife to find out if he'd gone home early. When he didn't turn up after a few more hours had passed, police arrived on the scene and began a preliminary investigation.

One of the detectives is quoted in the article as saying, "I'd like to say that I'm surprised by this turn of events, but I'm not. When you've got humans and vampires on staff in a closed facility, it's only a matter of time before that powder keg ignites and blows."

The writer of the article carefully stresses, in the final paragraph, that no one—vampire or human—is under suspicion of kidnapping at this point, but the anti-vampire protesters had assembled outside of the Give Life facility just after dawn, having somehow caught wind of the developing story. There's a photograph featuring five or six angry-faced humans holding up handmade signs reading *Go back to Transylvania* and *If you're with* them, *you're against* us.

I recognize Drew Yarrow at the front of the crowd.

And Mia, my girlfriend, with her long, dark hair drawn back into a ponytail, is standing nearby, one of the cardboard signs—*Vampires suck!*—clutched in her hands while she's gazing, puppy-dog-eyed, at Drew.

"Are you sure you don't want any popcorn?" Mia shakes the tub of buttered popcorn in her lap, her wide mouth curved up in a tempting, forbidden-fruit kind of smile.

"No, thanks." I slide down a little further in the cushy movie theater seat, my hands clenched on the armrests at my sides. I *want* to cross my arms over my stomach, thus preventing Mia from entwining her fingers with mine, but that would be childish and sulky of me, and I'm trying my best to remain even tempered. I made up my mind after I saw Mia's photo in the newspaper this afternoon that I wouldn't fling any accusations at her; I wouldn't even ask her if she spent the night with Drew— though, considering the fact that she attended the SANG meeting last night and then participated in a hate-mongering protest with

77

SANG in the wee hours of the morning, she probably did.

Maybe they stayed up all night talking, discussing the complicated moral issues involved in the anti-vampire movement.

Or...maybe Mia and Drew had sex.

As if illustrating my thoughts on film, the actor and actress onscreen exchange witty banter and begin to undress one another — tie, shirt, dress, bra. Soon enough, they're both naked and rolling around on a forest green-and-maroon hotel comforter.

I frown petulantly. Why are cheap hotel rooms *always* decorated in forest green and maroon?

"Courtney..." I stiffen as Mia suddenly takes my hand, pressing it to her butter-slick lips. "You look gorgeous tonight," she whispers into my ear, grazing her mouth over my goosebumped neck. "God, I hope this movie isn't long... I can't stand being near you without touching you." She slides one hand, with expert stealth, along my thigh and beneath the hemline of my dress.

Despite my many and varied inner conflicts, my body responds to her husky, sexy voice and her confident touch as it always does, always has: by getting incredibly hot and bothered. My heart is a hummingbird, beating, beating, and I feel my defenses, slowly but surely, begin to fall...

Be strong, Courtney.

That's what Azure told me after I showed her the newspaper photo and mentioned that I'd be seeing Mia tonight: "Be strong, Courtney. I wouldn't be best friends with a doormat. Doormats are tacky and gross. *You* aren't tacky and gross. You're stylish and hot. Plus, doormats are indiscriminate. They welcome every Tom, Dick and Harriet—even if Tom stepped in dog poop; Dick is, well, a dick; and Harriet pokes holes in the rubber with her high-heeled spikes.

"Be discriminating, Courtney.

"Be exclusive.

"You.

"Are.

"Not.

"A.

"Flipping.

"Doormat.

"So don't act like one!"

I'm pretty sure Azure would have carried on with the doormat analogies for half an hour longer, given the opportunity, but she had a dentist appointment and clocked out of work half an hour early.

Mia's fingers work their way along my inner thigh, her unpainted nails grazing my lacy pantyline. We're sitting in the back row of the movie theater, and the place is nearly empty, anyway: there are some necking teenagers a few rows in front of us, and an old woman is sitting alone in one of the aisle seats. So when Mia slides her fingertips beneath my panties and touches—ever so slightly—my wet center, I moan softly and bite my lower lip.

"Wanna go, baby?" she whispers, pressing harder against me.

"Yeah," I breathe, sighing as she, slowly, teasingly, draws her hand away. "Yeah, let's go. I think..." I swallow, slinging my purse strap over my shoulder, fighting against my longing as I pull my dress back into place. *Be strong. I am not a doormat. Or a throw rug. Or a floor runner. Or...anything else people track muddy footprints on.* "I think we need to talk, Mia."

📖

Before she took me to dinner and the movie, Mia gave me flowers. She appeared on my doorstep with a sly smile, her straight, dark hair loose and gleaming over her shoulders, her arms full of two dozen white roses.

Seated across from Mia, I gaze at the bouquet of twenty-four roses now and sigh bleakly. In the center of my kitchen table, stuffed into a too-small, chipped glass vase, they don't look elegant so much as...desperate. Strangled. Some of the petals have already fallen; Colette is batting at one of them on the tiled floor.

White roses used to be my favorite flower, but now I associate them with bad memories, painful moments. It's a sad but irrefutable truth that Mia only gives me flowers when she's nervous about discussing something personal with me or feeling guilty about her attraction to another woman. More often...the latter. And it's ironic, because white roses symbolize innocence, pure and unsullied love.

Over the course of our relationship, they've come to mean something else entirely: a pretty facade distracting attention from the sharp, scary, lurking thorns.

"What's up, baby? You look sad. Did something upsetting happen at the shop today?"

I shake my head, and the scent of the roses assaults my nose, sickly sweet. My stomach turns uneasily as I lift my gaze to meet Mia's narrowed brown eyes. "No, this has nothing to do with work. Mia..." I hold her stare. I promised myself I'd be receptive and frank during this conversation, so I state my cause simply, bluntly: "I don't know if this is working anymore."

She stills, blinks, parts her lips. "*This*?" she asks quietly—though, by her tone of voice, I can tell that she knows exactly what I mean.

"Yeah. This. Us," I force myself to say, wringing my hands in my lap. My stomach turns again.

"Oh." She bows her head. Some long

strands of hair have fallen loose from her ponytail, and they trail over the high planes of her pink-tinged cheeks. "Oh," she says again, her voice soft and faraway.

Normally, she sounds so certain, so persuasive that you can't help but hang on her every word, believe her fully, and go along with whatever scheme she suggests. In April, she talked me into skinny-dipping in a snapping turtle-infested, half-frozen creek—and I can't swim. The water was algae green and smelled like something rotting, but Mia made the experience feel exciting, sexy.

Now...she looks defeated, and she sounds so young. So small. Lost. *I* did this to her.

My heart shreds.

"You aren't happy with me, Courtney?"

"Are *you* happy, Mia?"

"I...I don't know. I thought we were having fun—"

"I *have* had fun with you." I reach for her hand across the table. She gives it to me; her fingers are damp and as cold as ice. When I'm upset, I go hot all over. Mia breaks out into a cold, clammy sweat. "A lot of fun." I draw in a deep breath. "But I've had a lot of heartache, too. Mia, I don't think I'm...enough for you. I don't satisfy you—"

"That isn't true. It's just... Courtney, I know I've been stupid and... I know I've hurt you, and that's the last thing I ever intended to do. But I can be different." She squeezes my hand hard. "I can change, baby. I lost my way for a little while. That's all. You know I've been stressed out at work—"

"No, I don't want you to change for me—"

"Not for you. For me. I want to be a better person. I want to be worthy of you, Courtney."

"Mia—"

"Give me another chance. I love you, baby." With her free hand, she strokes my cheek tenderly. Her brown eyes are watery, shining. "I love you so much. I've never loved anyone like this before, I swear. I messed up, but I can fix it, us; I can fix everything. Just let me try. Please, baby. You've got to let me try. Let me make you feel adored, worshiped." She rises from her chair and steps around the table until she's standing in front of me. Then she kneels down at my feet. Kneels down just like Lare had last night... "Let me make you feel like the goddess you are."

"Mia, I'm not a—" But I never finish my sentence, because she places her cool hands on my knees and begins to slide my dress up, up...and she bends her head toward me, trailing hot, lingering kisses over my inner thighs. "Oh, God, Mia," I breathe, as her mouth moves higher, closer. "Wait—"

"Do you want me to stop?" she whispers,

lifting her dark head to gaze hungrily into my eyes. "I'll stop—"

"Mia..."

Be strong, Courtney.
I am not a doormat.
I am not a...not a... I am... Mia's fingers tease at the edge of my panties.

"No, don't. Don't stop..."

Smiling wickedly but somehow sweetly, she lowers her mouth again.

Chapter Four: All the Right Places

Four days later—the prior forty-eight hours being comprised mostly of working and angsting; shamed by my carnal weakness, I've been avoiding Mia's calls—I finally get a bite on my Maximinus queries.

The email is brief and to the point, and from a contact of a contact, someone named Gustav in Hamburg, Germany:

To the proprietor of Banks' Books,
I have in my possession one of the few existing copies of a slender volume titled Biological Alchemy. *This book references the alchemist Maximinus on forty-nine pages. One chapter is entirely devoted to his research. Since, as I said, the book is very rare, I could not part with it for less than $20,000. Please contact me at this email address with your client's offer.*

Regards,
Gustav Reigle
Professor of Occult Sciences

"Wow, $20,000?" Azure says, whistling as she reads over my shoulder. "Steep."

"Yeah." I tap my finger on the mouse thoughtfully. "Hang on." I do a quick Google search for *Biological Alchemy* and come up with nothing, not a single mention of the book on all of the Internet. I return to the email tab and frown. "Well, it's the only lead we've got."

"I hope Lare's loaded."

Quickly, I send off a reply to Professor Reigle, requesting some photographs of the book and a condition description. I don't know if Lare has $20,000 to burn, but even if she does, I want to make sure this book is the real deal before I get her hopes up. Gustav Reigle is a professor, not a bookseller. To cover my bases, I send him a follow-up email, requesting character references.

"Well, I'm going to take off, boss," Azure says suddenly.

"What?" I swivel around in the chair to face her. She has her backpack slung over her shoulder, her yellow motorcycle helmet dangling from one hand.

"Today's my short day, remember? I've got a rehearsal at the fairgrounds for the music fest." She glances at her watch and shakes her head. "David was supposed to be here fifteen minutes ago to finish the shift. Sorry, but I'll be late if I don't set out now. Is it okay?"

"Sure. Of course. Go sing your heart out," I smile, waving a hand at her. "The shop's as quiet as a tomb today, anyway."

"Oh, God, don't talk about *tombs*." Azure closes her eyes and shivers. "I watched this creepy documentary last night about a house built on a graveyard. Everyone who lived in the place ended up dead or crazy. And my apartment building is right *next* to the old St. Michael's Cemetery. What if the contractor *accidentally* built on top of some unmarked graves?" Azure's eyes, outlined in thick black liner, widen as she stares at me. "I couldn't sleep a wink all night. I kept hearing this, like, *moaning*..."

I give her a wry smile. "Sure it wasn't Oliver having a bad dream?" Oliver is Azure's elderly collie.

"Come to think of it..." She tilts her head, considering. "Oliver *does* moan like a ghost whenever he's hungry. Bow-wow-woooow," she imitates, grinning. "Yeah, I'm just going to cling to that explanation." She backs toward the door. "Thanks, Court. I'm so gullible when it comes to spooky stuff. Part of me wants it to be true, I guess. But sometimes I need a skeptic's point of view — for my sanity's sake."

There's that word again — *skeptic*. I smile weakly. "Have fun at rehearsal."

"Have fun reading *Jane Eyre*. You *are* still reading it, right? Or should I hit your hands with a ruler and give you a pop quiz?"

I laugh, rising to pick up the store copy of the book from the desktop. "I'm reading it, you old schoolmarm. And I've read it before, you know."

"Read it, but you never *studied* it like the sacred tome that it is. You'll become a connoisseur of romance yet!" Azure blows me a kiss and then flies through the door, the bells jangling to announce her exit.

David calls in sick a few minutes after she leaves, complaining of a "stomach thing." I hired 19-year-old David Reynolds as a part-time employee about a year ago, before Randolph Palmer's sales took off. I don't begrudge anyone success, but the fact of the matter is that Randolph's success has hurt my business, and if my numbers don't level out soon, I'll be forced to consider the wisdom in keeping Banks' Books' doors open—and two employees on staff.

By closing time three hours later, I've waited on only one customer—a college kid looking for a copy of *Don Quixote* for her Spanish Literature class—and played seventy-three games of computer Solitaire. All of which I lost.

Jane Eyre lies unread and accusatory beside my mouse. I slide the book into my purse—I have several copies at home, but this one is illustrated *and* annotated, a literary nerd's dream—and then shut off the lights, locking the shop door behind me.

It's a bake-a-cake-and-eat-the-entire-thing-while-watching-sappy-lesbian-movies sort of evening.

The only trouble is...I'm out of sugar. Because I made a coconut cream pie last night. And I made double-chocolate brownies the night before.

Some people self-medicate with alcohol or drugs. I drown my sorrows in sugary baked goods.

"Be back in a minute," I tell Colette uselessly; she's too busy stalking a dust bunny to notice my long-faced comings and goings.

I grab my wallet and car keys and step outside into the humid evening air. I changed into a white tank top and jean shorts when I got home from work, but I still feel overdressed and overheated. Colonel Mustard's AC is on the fritz, so when I fall into the driver's seat, I unwind the window all the way and—squeezing one eye shut—jam the key into the ignition.

A rumble...a shudder...a weird sort of grinding noise...

And then nothing.

I sigh and sag against the seat, banging the back of my head against the headrest.

"Car trouble?"

Okay, knifing incident aside, I'm not a screamer, I swear. But in my current state of frustration—emotional, sexual, automobile, and otherwise—I'm caught off guard by the unexpected question and can't help but scream...a little.

Actually, it's more like a squeak.

"Sorry, Courtney. I didn't mean to startle you."

I swallow, gazing up into Lare's silver-blue eyes. *God, she's beautiful.* She's dressed in running shorts and a tight, sleeveless gray shirt, and red waves spill over her bare right shoulder. Her mouth is curved up into a concerned smile.

And there's a giant, slobbery, brown-and-white dog panting at her side. Van Helsing, I remember. He licks my car door thoughtfully before sprawling on the ground, plunking his enormous head down on his enormous paws.

"My car's a lemon," I explain to Lare, smiling up at her. "I was going to bake a cake, but I ran out of sugar. And old Colonel Mustard here"—I smack the steering wheel with my palm—"isn't quite up for a grocery store run. Maybe it's for the best, though. I've been...overindulging in the sweets department."

"There's no such thing as overindulging." She winks, and I can feel my body melting. "Besides..." Lare laughs, revealing those pointed teeth. "I know it's a cliché to borrow a cup of sugar from your neighbor, but clichés only exist because they reflect reality, right? So what do you say? Want some of my sugar, girl-next-door?"

My heart somersaults.

Did she really just...offer me her *sugar*?

Okay, I realize she meant it literally rather than, um, *another way*, but I still feel as I've just stumbled into an exploitative '80s hair band music video.

I pause. Then I shake my head and blink, confused. "Wait. I don't... You mean, you have sugar? In your house? I thought..." *Another vampire misconception, Courtney?* But I did read somewhere that vampires don't require food or water to survive...

"I don't eat like you do. That's true." Lare's mouth slants to one side. "But I like to keep my pantry stocked—in case any beautiful humans knock on my door." She gives me a meaningful look, and I flush beneath her stare. "Hospitality, you know. My foster family was human, so I picked up some cooking skills."

"Oh," I say hoarsely. "You had a foster family?"

She nods, still smiling, though there are dark gray shadows in her silver eyes. "But that was a long time ago." Pointing her gaze toward the dog at her feet, she sighs before meeting my stare again. "We've just been for a run around the neighborhood. Poor Helly's exhausted." Chuckling softly, she leans toward my car door and whispers, "As a cat owner, you may not know this, but dogs make excellent scapegoats. Blame them when *you're* exhausted after a run, and they'll never take it personally. Excellent pals, dogs. Always willing to help you save face *and* impress pretty ladies." She winks at me again. My blush deepens: pretty sure my skin color has progressed from watermelon pink to bright tomato red. My face feels as if it's generating enough heat to warm a large igloo.

Lare winds Helly's leash around her pale wrist. "Anyway, if you do decide to *indulge,* after all," she grins, "my door's right over there." She points, smiles coaxingly at me, and then jogs off in the direction of her one-story brick house.

I sit behind the wheel for a full minute, weighing the pros and cons of accepting Lare's invitation. It's what I do best: making lists. But, honestly, it's been a rough day, I'm overheated and experiencing sugar withdrawal, and I'm just not in a listmaking mood.

So, drawing in a deep breath, I work up the nerve to step out of the car and walk up Lare's flagstone sidewalk. There's a small grapevine wreath decorated with sprigs of blue flowers hanging on the door. I lift my hand to knock—

And Lare opens the door quickly, her smile warming me from the inside out. "Well, hello there, neighbor." She leans against the frame and offers me a coy grin, crossing her arms over her chest. "Now...how might I help you?"

Her smile is infectious—along with her playfulness. I duck my head. "I was wondering—I know it's cliché, but... Could I borrow a cup of sugar?"

"Oh, have the whole jar," she laughs, stepping aside and gesturing with her be-ringed hand. She's wearing a large ring with a black stone on her pointer finger, and another—shaped like a swan's head—on her thumb. "Please step into my lair." She grins. "I've always wanted to say that. You're my first visitor here, you know."

My heart tumbles in my chest as I move past her and into the dove gray entryway. Ninety-five percent of my involuntary instincts are telling me to turn around right now, to leave, to *save* myself from a certain...uncertainty. But the other five percent wins out—because logic tells me that vampires have more to fear from humans than humans do from vampires. There have only been a handful of vampire attacks on humans reported since the President went public, while the number of human attacks on vampires is, it seems, incalculable—and constantly on the rise.

If Lare trusts me enough to let me into her home, her sanctuary, that's important. That means something to me. I don't know, *can't* know what it's like to live life as a vampire, as a non-human, but I do know what it feels like to be the black sheep of the neighborhood, to wonder if the next knock at the door is going to bring you a warm casserole or a religious pamphlet and a defamatory speech.

I feel wretched now for having doubted her motivations last night, for having suspected—if only for a moment—that she wanted to drink my blood. The fact that she hasn't shunned me for my ignorance is proof of her innate goodness. She had every right to call me out for questioning her offer of help...but she didn't. She gave me another chance, a chance I really didn't deserve.

As she closes the door behind us, I catch her distinctive scent on the air: sweetness and flowers and something else, something deep and sensual. Not perfume. I think it's just...*Lare*. Lare, with her languid, art nouveau grace; with her raw, friendly, natural allure... Entirely natural, because there is no human-luring pheromone. Over the past few days—secretly and a little shamefully—I've Googled vampires nonstop, cramming my head with facts and figures, theories and truths. And I've discovered that the pheromone rumor is just that—a rumor. There is no scientific proof for its existence whatsoever.

So that means that what I'm feeling for Lare isn't the result of preternatural bait. My attraction is just...attraction. Intense, insistent, soul-deep attraction. This...pull. Like a magnet. Like Rochester and Jane's string.

"I'm sorry." I offer her an apologetic smile, bending over to pet Helly's scruffy brown-

and-white head. He laps at my hand appreciatively. "My neighborliness rating is in the red. I should have brought you a housewarming gift."

"Hey, my house is warm enough. Broken AC unit." Then she winks at me again and turns away. "Besides, your being here is a gift," she tells me over her shoulder, leading me (and Helly) into the small but charming kitchen. The walls are soft yellow, the cabinets scalloped and white, and there's a cream-colored tablecloth on the small table in the breakfast nook. She nods toward it. "Have a seat, Courtney."

"Okay. Thanks." I step over the old hardwood floor, pull out a chair and lower myself into it, awkwardly resting an elbow on the tabletop. "The house looks nice. Cozy. You've already unpacked?"

"Well, a little. The former owners sold me the place fully furnished. So most of this stuff"—she points to the Van Gogh sunflowers framed on the wall—"came with the deal. It suits me, though. I'm not much of a decorator. At my last place, I slept on a futon and used overturned crates for chairs." She taps her forehead, giving me a wry look. "One of the perils of scientific pursuit. There's no room in my head for aesthetics. Though I can still appreciate a beautiful thing when I see it." Lare turns and regards me with a pensive smile. Then she opens a cupboard door and begins pushing around the tins and canisters until she finally says, "Aha!" and draws out a blue-and-white jar marked with the word *sucre—sugar* in French. "Here we are."

Leveling me with a soft, cool stare, Lare strides back toward the table and hands me the jar, which I take automatically, subconsciously, because I can't seem to stop staring at her. I can't look away from those eyes... In the bright kitchen light, they're as blue as ice floes, as deep, as dangerous as the Arctic Ocean. Not silver, but not human, either: they're too lovely, too knowing, too penetrative and complicated to belong to a simple mortal being. I swallow and lick my lips, whisper, "Thanks," as I place the jar on the table.

"Sweets to the sweet," she smiles, arching a brow. "And I do expect you to use up the entire jar," she tells me, in her low, velvety tones. "Don't return it until you've spoiled your sweet tooth criminally."

I laugh. "Deal."

"So." Her eyes flick to my bare forearm. "How's your cut?"

"Oh, fine. Nearly healed. Thanks for your help."

"All the same," she says, voice dropping lower, causing my heart rate to dangerously accelerate, "I'd like to check up on it. If you don't mind."

Before I can respond, Lare crouches in

front of me, one knee pressed to the floor, the other hot against my leg. She's close, so close that...

I draw in a deep breath. I keep forgetting to do that: *breathe*. My heart is skip-skip-skipping in my chest. It skips another beat, then two, as Lare reaches between us, cradling my wrist in her long, deft fingers. They're so warm against my skin, her fingers, feather-light but sure. Practiced. Doctor's fingers.

She turns my hand over so that my wrist is exposed to her, and she brushes her dark-painted nails along my skin until she reaches the Band-Aid that I stuck on in place of the gauze. "Sorry, this might sting..." But she peels the sticky thing aside gently, stinglessly, and bends her head, lips parted, to consider my little wound.

Dry-mouthed, I gaze at the top of her head, at her hair beneath the overhead light; the thick strands shine red and gold, waterfalling over her china-smooth, bare shoulders. Her scent surrounds me. I could reach up with my free hand, could thread my fingers through her hair and trace the shell-like curve of her ear, feel the warmth of her cheek beneath my shaky fingertips...

"It's healing well," Lare murmurs, lifting her gaze with a small, secretive smile. Her voice jars me out of my reverie. "You won't have to worry about scarring."

"Oh." My voice is gravelly, and my head feels kind of gravelly, too: rough, overcrowded, disoriented. "Great."

She rises in her silent, tiger-like way and regards me with eyes too blue to compare to anything belonging to the natural world. They're alight, alive, *neon*. "Now, would you like some tea?" Lare leans on the table, her right thigh bumping—again, feather-light—against my knee. "It's hot out there. You must be thirsty."

"Thirsty?" I stammer, swallowing as my eyes skip to her mouth, flit over her sharp, bared teeth. *How does she kiss?* I wonder, blushing at the thought. *How does it feel to be kissed by her, to feel those teeth against your teeth, those lips against your lips, those long white arms wrapped around you...*

My heart thumps loudly in my chest.

Okay.

I'm kind of a mess.

I cough and smile at her self-consciously. "I wouldn't want you to go to any trouble—"

"No trouble. It's vanity. I make my own tea blends and am always eager to find new and willing victims—er, tasters." She grins and tilts her head to one side, red waves tumbling over her arm. "Because I can't taste them myself, of course."

"Right." I bite my lip, taking this in. Vampires can't eat, can't drink anything aside from blood. My brows narrow. "But then...why do you make them?"

"Mm, the million-dollar question." Her mouth slides into a slow, easy smile. "As a scientist and, well, a *vampire*, choosing and combining the ingredients, hypothesizing how those ingredients might taste together, and then conducting tea-drinking experiments with friends and colleagues, is an oddly satisfying—and relaxing—hobby. So much of my work is about hard things, big things—life, death. It's a comfort to mix herbal potions during my free hours. It feels a little bit like..." She glances off, her expression smooth and thoughtful. When she looks at me again, she's wearing this intense smile that makes my heart leap against the cage of my ribs. "Magic," she says softly, chuckling beneath her breath.

"Magic," I repeat, watching her, marveling at her. "You mean, like alchemy?" She glances at me in surprise. "Like that book you wanted me to look up?" I go on, breathless.

She laughs again. "Well...I'm not an alchemist. Or a magician. But I'm always chasing after that feeling. That...*numinousness.*" Her eyes fire like glittering aquamarines as her voice rises with her excitement. "Have you ever felt it? It's a—I don't know—*high* feeling, like you're disembodied and floating, like you know all of the secrets of the universe, but you can't *quite* put them into words..."

"Yeah," I say softly, nodding my head and licking my lips. I lean forward over the table, supporting my head on my hands as I gaze up into Lare's watchful, gleaming eyes. "When I read an especially moving or crushing or inspiring or...exquisitely phrased sentence in a book... Yeah. I feel it then. I feel weightless and a little dizzy—"

"That's it. That's it exactly. *Oui.* I knew you'd understand..." Lare lifts an arm to brush some hair back from her face, and as she moves, I stare at the tattoo on her wrist, at the large black V and the numbers imprinted beneath it: 45832. She pauses, noticing the direction of my gaze. "Pathetic, isn't it, as far as body modifications go?"

"What?" I glance up at her.

"My tattoo. When they made me get it, you know, I asked the tattoo...well, I don't know what to call them. I hesitate to use the word *artists.* But I asked the tattoo *people* if I could choose a different font for my brand, or a different color, but they refused to speak to me. They barely acknowledged my existence." Her eyes look distant, misty, as she smooths her thumb over the numbers on her arm. "I imagine that's what cattle feel like, hmm? Unpitied." Her voice is so soft, I can hardly hear her; maybe she doesn't want me to hear her.

I *do* hear her, though, and my heart aches with a sharp, deep pain. Because it's true. The vampire tattoo is an insult, a purposeful insult. It's humanity's way of marking the vampires as inferior, lesser creatures—lesser even than cattle. Cattle are wanted; by and large, vampires are not. Here in Cincinnati, there are only four Free Residence neighborhoods where vampires can move in without petitioning the residents first and proving themselves—through a series of humiliating tests—to be upright citizens. Some of the shops downtown have *Vampires not welcome* signs posted in their windows, and groups like SANG strive to make the vampires' lives more difficult—and more dangerous—than they already are.

I don't know how Lare endures it: the demoralization, the bare hatred.

Suddenly my small and very human problems seem, well, selfish and silly in comparison.

Suddenly I feel very ashamed of sharing genes with humanity—at this point in history, at least.

On instinct, I stand up beside Lare and place my hand over her tattoo, obscuring it with my palm and fingers. The skin of her arm is softer, warmer than her hands, and she doesn't startle at my touch, doesn't move away. She only tilts her gorgeous head of hair toward me, eyes icy pinpoints of light, and offers me a small, quizzical smile.

"I'm sorry we did this to you," I tell her,

my voice low and hoarse with emotion. "I never realized..." I curse beneath my breath. "I've been so stupid, Lare. So wrapped up in my safe little haven of books; I shut the rest of the world out. I've always done that. I've always...cocooned myself. When President Garcia told the world about vampires, I hardly noticed. I wasn't curious. I didn't give it more than a passing thought. *God.*" I rake a hand back through my hair.

Growing up, my sister used to tell me that I was too focused, forever staring into a metaphorical kaleidoscope. All I could see were the pictures right in front of my face—or, more often, the *book* right in front of my face. She would stand on her head and make silly faces and do all sorts of things to try to catch my attention...but I just kept reading.

That's how I've lived my life, I realize now. Every single aspect of it. Tunnel vision. Ignore the peripheries, ignore the relationship issues with Mia, because you might see something you don't want to see, or know, or acknowledge. Something too hard, too painful. And life is painful enough.

"I'm sorry," I say again, drawing a deep breath into my lungs and meeting Lare's bright, watchful eyes. I slide my hand to the back of her wrist, so that the tattoo is visible once more; I regard it bleakly, tracing a finger over the thick lines of the V. My sister is covered in tattoos, and none of her body art feels like this: Lare's skin is raised up beneath the ink, as if swollen. The tattooist obviously used a less-than-gentle hand—and, in all likelihood, less-than-sterile materials—when he or she imprinted Lare.

My breath comes out in a huff. "You don't deserve this. *No one* deserves to be treated like this."

"Courtney." Her long lashes lower to her cheeks. "I appreciate the sentiment, but this wasn't your doing. There's nothing to apologize for—"

"There is, though. Because I'm one of them. I'm human. And I never spoke up. I never protested. I never *understood*—"

"*Oui.*" Smoothly and slowly, Lare captures my hand with both of hers, cradling it in her palms. Her lips draw up into a sad, subtle curve. "But you understand now. That's all that matters. And it *does* matter. Very much." Her soft eyes search mine, alternately flashing blue, then silver. "It matters to me. Thank you."

"Don't thank me. I don't—"

"Shh." Lare places a finger against my lips; my eyes widen with surprise, and my heart does a backflip in my chest. "I don't want an apology from you. You don't represent all of humanity any more than I represent all of vampirekind. We're just two *people*, Courtney, aren't we? Two people who have more in common than geography. Two people who

103

enjoy books, and conversation, and one another's company..." Her gaze flits over my mouth as she draws her finger away.

I swallow, sliding my hands into the back pockets of my shorts. It's a reflexive gesture, but there's a reason for it. If I didn't purposefully put my hands in my pockets, I would reach up right now, reach for her, and I shouldn't... I *can't*. I take another deep breath. "You...enjoy my company?" I ask her, feeling childish and the *opposite* of suave: *Do you like me? Check yes or no.*

But I don't have to wait very long for my answer. "Very much," Lare says again, taking a step nearer to me, filling the empty space that had lingered between us. I feel her hands lightly grip either side of my hips and, startled, I search her eyes. They're fully silver now, her eyes—two mirrors reflecting my flushed, confused face and my hair: a bright, tangled mess.

Lare's lips part, revealing her sharp incisors. But there's nothing menacing in her expression; those teeth are simply a part of her, and I can't imagine her without them. I don't want to imagine her without them. "Do you enjoy *my* company, Courtney?"

God, yes. I want to kiss her. I've never wanted to kiss anyone as much as I want to kiss Lare right here, right now. The feeling is so raw, so all-consuming, so primal, that I clench my teeth and fist my hands to force it down, to restrain my instinct—though my heart still beats like a frenetic drum inside of me, and my blood feels too hot, too *aware*...

"Well?" Lare smiles, arching a brow.

"You...fascinate me," I tell her truthfully, flushing more deeply with every word. "Yes. Yes, I enjoy your company. I... I feel like a different person whenever I'm around you."

She chuckles lightly. "And is that a good thing?"

"It's an amazing thing. It's...a really good thing."

Lare laughs again, a low, husky vibration that I feel in every nerve center of my body. "All right, then. I suppose there's only one thing left for us to do."

I swallow and bite my lower lip, unable to tear my eyes away from the beautiful, full curve of her mouth. "What should we do?"

"Well, toast to our friendship, of course," she says simply. Her words suggest platonic affection, but her tone of voice—and that hot glint in her eyes—suggests...otherwise, and an electric current moves through me, jump-starting my sleepy soul. "So, Courtney," Lare breathes, leaning near, her hands still poised quite naturally on my hips, "would you like a glass of iced tea?"

"I'd love one," I answer quickly, mentally transposing the words *a glass of iced tea* with *a night of passion*...

But Lare was, of course, being literal. A moment later, she hands me a tall glass of a faintly pink liquid, its surface bobbing with ice cubes that reflect the light. "Lavender green tea, with hints of rose petals, hibiscus and jasmine. I call it the Oscar Wilde," she smiles, watching me take a sip.

The flavor is, at first, subtle, but then a soft, floral sweetness dances over my tongue, and my eyes widen as I swallow another cool gulp. "Lare—what did you put in this, the nectar of the gods? Or, I don't know, *booze*?"

She laughs and shakes her head, her coppery waves catching the light. "I just did science to it," she grins, with a wink. "That's a new blend I've been working on; you're my first taster. So how would you rate it, on a scale of one to five stars?"

"A hundred stars, and—honestly—I'm not a tea drinker. I mean, I enjoy a cup now and then, but I guzzle coffee like cars guzzle gasoline. This, though..." I gaze at the half-empty glass in my hand. "It's like drinking flowers and *energy* at the same time. I was exhausted a moment ago, in my car, and now I feel like..." I pause, lips parted, as my eyes move over Lare's long, artful length. She's leaning back against the refrigerator door (which is bare, I realize now, save for one pulp fiction-style magnet declaring *How come all the cool girls are lesbians?*), arms crossed over her low-swooping tank top, watching me with the quiet, receptive, concentrated gaze of a scientist, a doctor, a lover.

"You feel like what, Courtney?" she prompts me softly.

"I..." I draw in a shallow breath and, with shattering regret, remind myself that I am *not* a single woman—regardless of the fact that my flighty girlfriend might be doing God-knows-what right now with God-knows-who. I want Lare... I want her with a passion I didn't know I was capable of feeling. It's heart-seizing; it's bone deep. But I need to break things off with Mia, once and for all, before I even begin to wonder whether Lare might feel the same way about me. Lare's been warm and friendly and sweet and teasing, but I don't know her, not really. I don't know what she wants from a relationship, or if she wants a relationship at all.

Still, if that fridge magnet is any indication, my gaydar was spot on, and Lare is a member of a long (and exploitative—cinematically speaking) legacy of sapphic vampires. But for all I know, she might have a girlfriend, too.

"Courtney?"

I cough self-consciously. "Um, didn't you say something about a toast?"

"Oh... I did, didn't I?" Lare looks thoughtful for a moment; then she pushes off from the refrigerator door and grabs another tall, clear glass from the cabinet to her left. With a sheepish smile, she strides over to me. "Let's pretend my glass is half full, hmm?"

I blink. "You aren't drinking?"

"No, I can't drink tea—"

"Not tea. I mean..." God, my throat is dry. I lick my lips and meet Lare's confused gaze. "Blood," I say softly, swallowing. "You could fill your glass with blood—"

"Courtney, that's..." She watches me for a moment; then she sighs heavily. "No. I don't think that would be a good idea." She crosses her arms over her chest, still gripping the empty glass in her hand. "I've never... I couldn't. You wouldn't want to see—"

"I do, though," I tell her, and then cringe a little, because the statement sounds voyeuristic and a little ghoulish. But I'm asking her to drink in the interest of fairness. It isn't fair for me to drink and eat in mixed company and for her to be forced to hide her appetite away. That's like the right-wingers insisting that gay couples shouldn't kiss in public, because it might upset the straights.

It's discrimination.

"Please, Lare. It's only fair," I say, my voice wavery, quiet. "You have just as much right as me to—"

"I appreciate the sentiment, Courtney. I really do." She rakes a hand back through her red waves, uncertainty flickering in her silver stare. "But it's...a big deal. It's something I've always kept hidden. From my foster family, from friends. I don't even drink in front of other vampires."

"Oh." My eyes widen. "Oh, I'm sorry. I didn't mean to cross a line or...make you uncomfortable." My face flushes, and I stare at the floor, at my feet, Lare's feet. Her feet are bare, and the nails are painted a deep, chic charcoal gray. I inhale deeply. "I only wanted you to know... You don't have to hide with me. I...know some things about hiding." I smile weakly, blushing beneath her intense, thoughtful gaze. "And it sucks. It makes you feel like less than a person. I don't want you to feel that way." I take a step nearer to her, drawing in another deep breath. "Not with me."

For a long, tense moment, Lare doesn't reply. She stares hard into my eyes, and I feel as if her gaze has moved through my outer surfaces and into my soft, secret core. I'm too hot, too bewildered, but I don't glance away from her, can't glance away and break this electric, gossamer thread drawn taut between us.

Then her mouth slants subtly on one side, and she says, "I've never met anyone like you before."

"Like me?" I bow my head and chuckle. "Incredibly awkward and prone to inappropriate suggestions?"

But Lare shakes her head and reaches for my free hand. She's warm, so warm, and her touch is gentle but firm as she effortlessly weaves her fingers through mine. Her long nails graze against my palm; I shiver. "No. Incredibly kind and prone to surprising acts of empathy." She's standing close enough that I can make out faint freckles on her nose and cheeks; her sweet, lily scent is the only air I breathe. She squeezes my hand, and a thousand pinpricks of pleasure needle my skin, causing me to shiver again. "Are you sure it wouldn't bother you?"

"I'm sure," I whisper. Then I clear my throat and say it once more, louder this time: "I'm sure. But I don't want to pressure you into doing something that makes you uneasy. We hardly know each other—"

"Oh, hardly?" She smiles, letting go of my hand and pressing it over her heart, feigning hurt feelings. "And I thought we were beginning to know each other quite well."

"We are." I smile back at her. "I just meant that we haven't known one another for very long, and I understand if you don't trust me enough to—"

"I trust you."

It's my turn to place a hand over my heart; I feel it beating hard beneath my fingertips, frenzied, and I'm acutely, painfully aware of the fact that it has never beat like this for Mia—or for anyone else. "I trust you, too, Lare."

"*Bon.* Well, then..." She opens the refrigerator door and removes a black plastic packet, rectangular and about the size of a pasta box. After one adorably nervous glance back at me over her shoulder, she moves to the countertop, opens the packet and pours its contents into her empty glass. When she turns to face me again, she's holding the glass in her left hand, obscuring most of it with her fingers and palm, but she can't hide it completely. The thick liquid rises up to the top and is dark red, almost black, beneath the kitchen's bright lights.

Lare raises the glass slightly; I notice that her hand is shaking. "Shall we?" she asks, tilting her glass toward mine.

I clink the rim of my iced tea against Lare's cold glass of blood.

"To neighbors," I say, gazing deeply into her silver-blue eyes.

"To power outages and sugar outages." A slow smile claims her mouth. "For bringing neighbors together."

I blush.

Then, in silence, we drink.

Despite my assertions, I admit that I worried watching Lare drink blood might trigger some ancient, genetic flight-or-fight mechanism in my subconscious brain...but it doesn't. As I gulp down my flower-flavored tea, Lare takes sips from her glass—little sips, dainty sips, never spilling a drop. And it isn't creepy or even strange. In fact, after she's drunk half the glass, her shoulders noticeably relax, and her face takes on a rosier hue. I can feel waves of heat emanating from her body as her eyes hold mine, flashing mirror bright.

In her newly fortified aura, my own body feels as if it's on fire. My fingers are flames; my tongue is a lash of lightning. I find myself leaning toward her, face burning... And she leans toward me, too, her lips parted, her teeth speckled with flecks of wet blood.

The tea glass slides out of my grasp and breaks on the kitchen floor with a spectacular, horrifying crash.

"Oh, my God—"

"It's all right. I'll get the broom—"

"No, let me sweep it up, please. And I'll replace your glass. I'm so sorry."

Smiling gently, Lare places her own glass on the countertop and produces a broom and dustpan from the side of the refrigerator. "Glasses break, Courtney. It's one of life's certainties. Here." She hands me a long-handled broom and then crouches down on the floor before me. "You sweep, and I'll hold the dustpan. Teamwork, okay?"

"Right. Teamwork," I mutter, silently cursing my clumsiness as I carefully gather the shards of broken glass with the rough bristles. Helly's snoring (loudly) beside the kitchen table, so at least there's no danger of him stepping on the glass and injuring his gigantic paws.

Well, maybe this is fate's way of staging an intervention to prevent me from cheating on my all-too-human girlfriend with my all-too-alluring vampire neighbor.

Or maybe—and more likely—I'm just a flailing, utterly hopeless *disaster*.

A hopeless disaster with all kinds of *feelings* she can't neatly categorize or label. Feelings she's never, ever had to sort through before.

I sigh, frustrated, as Lare empties the dustpan full of glittery glass pieces in the trashcan beneath the sink. "Would you like some more iced tea?" she asks.

"No. No... We shouldn't risk it." I wave my fingers in the air and smile weakly. "Don't let these butter fingers anywhere near the rest of your glassware. Or bakeware. Or, hell, Tupperware—just to be safe."

Lare meets my eyes, but she doesn't return my smile; her mouth is a straight, thoughtful line. In three easy strides, she's standing before me, taking the broom from my hand and then holding onto my hand herself, trailing her thumb over the backs of my knuckles. "Courtney," she says quietly, murmuring my name in her soft French accent, "why do you do that?" Her silver-blue eyes chase after my flitting gaze like glinting stars.

"Do what?" My voice is barely a whisper.

"Insult yourself." She shakes her head, red waves shifting over her shoulders and brushing lightly against the planes of my cheeks. "You're a successful businesswoman with a wicked sense of humor and a sharp intellect. And you're beautiful. You're the most beautiful woman I've ever met." Her eyes flash as they bore into mine. "Or, I'm certain, ever will."

I try to swallow, but my tongue is suddenly four sizes too big, and my throat feels tight and constricted. My heart, on the other hand, is having no difficulty performing its assigned functions—albeit at four times the speed of light. For a moment, I entertain serious concerns that it might thump itself right out of my chest.

"Lare," I say, and then I pause, speechless, and shake my head.

"It's an honor to know you, Courtney. I only wish you cherished yourself as much as other people cherish you. It's a lesson I've had to learn myself, and it was difficult...but well worth the effort."

Cherish. I think about that word, think about it for, perhaps, the very first time, and I grow still. It's a word you don't often hear outside of wedding ceremonies and that old Madonna song. And now, considering it, *cherish* feels like the word I've been searching for my entire life, the word I've always wanted to put into action in my relationships: *to cherish; to be cherished...*

Do I cherish Mia? Does she cherish me? I can't answer either question positively without hesitation, and that makes my stomach flutter with a sickening, winged dread.

I bite my lip as I inhale deeply. "Well," I say, breathing out, "self-esteem baggage aside...it's an honor to know you, too, Lare. Thank you for being so"—I chuckle, amused by the inadequacy of the word—"neighborly. I haven't really gotten to know my neighbors, despite living here for years. So it's nice to..."

She watches me expectantly, a faint smile shadowing her lips.

"It's nice to have a friend next door," I say, my gaze moving again to the tattoo on her wrist.

For a moment, Lare holds her tongue, silent, as her thumb makes semicircles on the back of my hand. Then she sighs lightly. "*Oui*. It's a comfort for me, too, knowing you're so close. A strange comfort. I've been alone for most of my life."

I meet her sad, hooded stare.

"So, *merci*," she says, mouth slanting up slightly on one side, "for giving the new vampire on the block the benefit of the doubt." Her sexy smile gives way to parted lips and flashing eyes. "That means a lot to me, Courtney." She licks her lips, holding my gaze. Her own gaze glitters with something private, unspoken. "Much more than you might think."

She weaves her fingers with mine.

I take a step closer.

And a piercing whine breaks the tension between us—as Lare breaks physical contact with me. "I'm sorry. That's my pager."

"People still have pagers?"

She smiles at me over her shoulder as she jogs into the entryway; when she returns, she's cradling a small white device in her hand. It's making a high-pitched wail, and she clicks a button on it as she skims the small screen, mouth tensing into a straight line.

"Is everything all right?" I ask.

"No. No, it isn't. I...I have to go." She looks up at me and meets my gaze, but she isn't really seeing me: her eyes are faraway, elsewhere. "I'm sorry, Courtney." She blinks—once, twice—and then she's back again, staring into me, her mouth curved in a soft, regretful half-smile. "There's a...situation at work. I'm afraid I'm needed there. I had hoped we could..."

I wait for her to finish her sentence, but she only shakes her head, placing a hand to her brow.

"Oh, before you go—here." Picking up a tin painted with yellow roses from the countertop, Lare removes the lid and chooses something from the inside; then she smiles at me and presses that something into my hand.

"Another new recipe. Let me know what you think of it, all right?"

I look at the plastic-bagged tea packet in my hand. It has a neat label affixed to it, reading *Colette*.

"I just completed the recipe yesterday—inspired by your lovely cat."

Grinning, I tuck the tea packet into my shorts pocket. "Thanks. I'll drink it at work tomorrow. It'll give me something to look forward to."

"Good..." Lare glances at her beeper again and sighs. "I look forward to seeing more of you. Unfortunately, that's impossible tonight." She rakes her free hand through her red hair and sighs again, deeply. "So I'll have to bid you *au revoir*. Enjoy your cake, Courtney."

"What?" I shake my head, lost in Lare's silver-blue eyes. "Oh... Right. My cake. Yeah. Thanks again for the sugar." I pick up the canister, cradling it awkwardly in my arms.

Lare steps toward me and raises her hand; with slow, liquid movements, she brushes a strand of hair from my face, leaving the back of her hand against my cheek. "I bought it for you. I just didn't know that at the time." Her mouth slides into a small, apologetic smile. "Sometimes fate is a wonderful thing. And sometimes..." She takes her hand from my cheek and regards the device in her palm bleakly. "Sometimes it breaks your heart."

"I'm sorry. Do you need my help with anything? I could, I don't know, dogsit Van Helsing for you or—"

"Thanks, but I'll be back in a couple of hours. Helly the hellhound ought to be able to fend for himself until then," she says, with a hint of her usual good humor.

"Well, I hope everything works out. I'm...sorry that you have to deal with this." I step out of the kitchen and through the living room, toward the front door. "If I get any leads on that book, I'll give you a call."

"*Merci.* Good night, Courtney."

"Good night, Lare." I open the door, and the heat wafts in, damp and suffocating.

I walk down the sidewalk and onto the flagstones leading to my own house, and then, skin prickling, I glance over to my alluring neighbor's property. Lare is standing in the doorway, arms crossed over her chest, watching me; a complicated expression flits over her face. As I wave self-consciously, she smiles; then she backs into her house, shutting the door with a soft click.

After a lot of indecision, I end up baking a double-layer vanilla cake with raspberry filling and chocolate ganache, and I'm keenly aware with every bite of Lare's comment about the sugar: *I bought it for you. I just didn't know that at the time.* I've never known anyone who spoke so often and so naturally about woo-woo things like fate, destiny, kismet... And I've never put any credence in fate myself, because, if fate really is a force in my life, it's always been skewed towards the blah rather than the beautiful.

But as I watch *When Night is Falling* for the hundredth time and devour my decadent dessert with its sweet, borrowed sugar, I can't help but wonder if destiny might have something beautiful in store for me, after all.

Chapter Five: Definitely Not a Lunch Date

It's not until the following morning, when I'm polishing off an almond croissant and skimming email messages at the shop, that I realize I failed to tell Lare about the lead I received on her book search. Yesterday evening was...intense, but I should have shared the fact that my contact tracked down a book containing information on Maximinus the moment Lare jogged up to my car.

The thing is...that *ridiculously* rare and expensive book was the farthest thought from my mind when my hot vampire neighbor and her dog materialized outside of my window. I wasn't doing much thinking at all, frankly. And in the glaring light of day, with an email from Mia *glaring* at me from my inbox—the subject lines reads, *You, me, naked: soon?*--I feel wretched, sick with guilt. My gut is tangled up in knots. I almost regret eating that rich, sweet croissant for breakfast.

Almost.

I lick my fingers appreciatively, one by one.

Then I sigh and bang my skull on the counter before cradling my head on my arms.

Okay, time for a cold, hard fact, Courtney: it doesn't matter that Mia and I have been drifting apart lately. It doesn't even matter that she's got some weird thing for Drew Yarrow, or that she's become a hate sign-carrying, honorary member of SANG. As of right now, Mia and I are still in a relationship, still exclusive, committed to each other...and that means something to me. Something big.

But, as much as I cringe to admit it, there's a small part inside of me that...*doesn't* feel guilty about the time I've spent with Lare, or the sexy thoughts I've had about Lare. A small, strange, and *shockingly* uninhibited part inside of me that is kind of, sort of wishing Lare had never gotten that mysterious and urgent page from GLT. Because if she hadn't gotten the page... Well, after the intimate experience she and I shared—drinking together, trusting together, mortifying broken-glass incident aside—it felt wrong to sever our connection so abruptly. If she hadn't been summoned away, things might have progressed, deepened between us, and then...

And then what? In frustration, I sit up and close my laptop with a *click*. My droopy eyes fall to my cell phone, lying face-down in front of me on top of a pile of unopened mail. Unopened *bills*. Bills I can't quite afford to pay.

The knots in my stomach tighten.

Right.

Back to business, boss.

I sigh and pick up the phone gingerly, as if it might bare teeth and bite. It doesn't, but my hand is, to my dismay, shaking as I unlock the screen and draw Lare's business card out of a drawer. I suck in a deep breath and punch in the first few digits of Lare's number—and then my phone freezes up. And starts ringing. Or, rather, starts playing my ringtone, the theme song from Disney's *Beauty and the Beast.* It's been one of my favorite movies for years. My teenage self vaguely appreciated the fairy tale romance, I guess, but it was the sight of Belle's majestic library made my bibliophile heart skip a beat.

Now my eyes widen as I stare at the phone in my hand. The number flashing on the screen is Lare's, the same number I'd been in the process of entering myself.

That's...weird.

Dazed, I answer the phone, only dimly aware of my actions. "Hello?" I try to keep my voice even, calm and professional, but it comes out husky and hoarse, breaking on the *lo.* I clear my throat.

"Courtney? It's Lare," she tells me, *her* voice warm and soft, sensual and low. I can tell she's smiling, and a blush creeps over my body, turning my skin beet red from the chest up. I lean on the counter hard—my knees are, all of the sudden, too weak to support my weight—and try not to picture her mouth forming my name. Instead, I think of the tea that she poured me last night, its floral scent mingling with Lare's own lily-sweet perfume. I think about drinking with her. I think about how she brushed her fingernails over my forearm as she examined my wound...

Uh, not helping.

Earth to Courtney.

"Hi, Lare," I say, too loudly and too brightly, after I realize that she's been waiting several seconds for me to reply. I slog through the awkward pause with a grimace. "It's funny that you called, actually. I was just about to dial you." I rake a hand back through my hair. My palms are sweaty, and my heart is beating so fast that I find myself taking small, quick breaths to compensate. It's kind of unsettling.

I mean, I've *read* about characters getting all flustered over their "one true love," but I thought that was just literary technique, some sort of romantic, poetic exaggeration. Women used to swoon all of the time, according to period novels, but I've never seen anybody—female or otherwise—swoon in my entire life.

The surreal thing is...I kind of feel like I'm in danger of swooning every time I'm in Lare's company. Or even, apparently, just talking to her on the phone.

"You were really about to call me?"

"Yeah."

"Well..." She's still smiling; I can tell by the tone of her voice. But she sounds tired, too. Maybe she had a late night after we parted ways. "You must have heard me thinking about you, then. I suspect you're a little bit psychic, Courtney Banks," she teases.

In truth, I'm feeling a little bit psy*cho*, but I laugh noncommittally. "I do have this uncanny sixth sense for always going to the grocery store when it's so crowded that there aren't any shopping carts left. Kind of a superpower, I guess."

Her soft chuckle makes my stomach somersault. "Look," she says, in a velvet tone, "I wanted to apologize for last night. It was terribly rude of me to just—"

"No, please don't worry about it." I lick my lips and draw in a deep breath, weighing my next words. "I was just sorry that we had to cut our, um...teatime...short." I press the phone harder against my cheek as my eyes flit up toward the ceiling, fixing on a water stain that I hadn't noticed before. Lovely.

"I was sorry, too," Lare murmurs. "Sincerely sorry."

I swallow, then bite my lip. "So... Was everything all right? I mean, at GLT?"

"Well..." She's silent for a long moment; when she speaks at last, her voice is tight. "Yes. And no. But that's not important right now."

Her tone brightens, but I can still hear the strain beneath it. "I told myself that the moment I was free, I would call you and apologize. *And* — more importantly — offer reparations. Will you join me for lunch, Courtney, to make up for yesterday?"

Lunch? My eyes widen, and I stand very still. In one of the aisles of the currently customer-less bookstore, I can hear David dusting the shelves, whistling a tune I've never heard before. Its minor notes are haunting, eerie, and repetitive, like a witch hunter's anthem — or a vampire's lament.

My head feels as if it's stuffed with too much information, too many thoughts and counterthoughts, as I consider Lare's unexpected invitation.

What's the big deal? It's just lunch. Mia goes out to lunch with friends and interviewees all the time, nearly every day. Sometimes Azure and I grab a bite to eat after work. It's what friends do, eat together.

Of course, in this case, *I'll* be the only one eating...

I watch some dust motes, glittering in the sunlight, settle on the top of one of my latest acquisitions, a sumptuously illustrated, Victorian-era copy of *Pride and Prejudice*. And so I think, crazily, irrationally, *What would Jane Austen do?*

Well, obviously, Jane would accept a

lunch invite from a neighbor, because a refusal without valid cause would be deemed impolite and ungrateful.

Right?

So I'll accept to be polite and grateful. It's as simple as that. No ulterior motivations. No danger of feeling compelled by inappropriate romantic fantasies—

"Sure," I say, quickly and unthinkingly. I can't think, because if I do think, I'll remember Mia and have to confront the the fact that my desire to go to lunch with Lare has nothing to do with Regency etiquette and everything to do with my, well, desire. *For* Lare.

Yeah. Best to disable my inner Virgo right now and avoid thinking altogether.

After all, it *is* only lunch.

Lunch with a woman you're desperately attracted to.

I bite my lip again—*hard*.

"Oh, *bon*, that's wonderful. I'll see you around noon, then? In just a little while? You're at your shop, yes? I'm not far... I'll pick you up there," Lare tells me, her voice as warm as her skin.

Stop it, Courtney.

"Noon, yes. Yeah, perfect. I can't wait." And then, before I can say/do/think anything else, I end the call.

Dumfounded and startled, I place the phone on the counter, regarding its screen with a sort of mystic wonder.

I don't need a mirror to know that my cheeks are, tellingly and brightly, flushed. Thank God Azure isn't here right now to catch me red-handed—er, red-faced.

I curl my fingers around my *I read banned books* mug, lifting the chipped rim to my lips and inhaling, for the first time, the heady aroma of the tea that Lare gave me last night, that Lare created in honor of my cat. I know that glamorous fluffball doesn't appreciate the gesture, but I do. Tentatively, I take a sip.

On my tongue, the hot liquid is spicy and bold, with a decadent chocolate rise and a sweet cinnamon aftertaste. And there's...something else. I take another sip and tilt my head, considering.

Oh, my God, I know that scent...

I laugh out loud; my lips curl at Lare's cleverness.

Catnip. She put catnip in Colette's tea. Good thing I brought the packet to work, because Colette would ravage it if I left it anywhere in the kitchen. Some cats get all cute and roly-poly when they're high on catnip, but Colette gets downright destructive. When I first adopted her, I bought her a little blue mouse stuffed with catnip, and she not only tore that mouse apart, but she also chewed holes in the toes of my boots and dragged the blankets off of my bed. I found them in a pile at the bottom of the stairs when I woke up, shivering, in the morning.

Honestly, I think catnip is Colette's version of Popeye's spinach. It makes her crazy strong—or maybe just crazy.

Either way, Lare chose well.

As I down the rest of the contents of my mug, David walks by the front desk with a stack of books in his arms. He nods agreeably to me, still whistling that kind-of-creepy tune.

All in all, David Reynolds is a model employee: he completes his tasks—shelving, waiting on customers—quietly and without fuss. His level-headedness and his literary knowledge drove me hire him, and he hasn't ever disappointed me on either score. He has yet to open up about his personal life, so I don't know where he goes or what he does when he isn't at the store. And, really, that isn't my business. He's private but pleasant; we've always gotten along well as co-workers, and I know I can trust him to get his job done, and done well.

Still, there's something unnerving about this tune... It's kind of catchy, in a maddening, stuck-in-your-head-for-days way.

"Hey, David," I call after him, as he reaches up to shelve a gold-gilt edition of *Les Miserables.*

He pauses, glancing my way in surprise.

"What's that song you're whistling?" I smile. "I don't think I'm familiar with it."

"Sorry. Was I bothering you?" His brown eyes flicker as he fumbles with the heavy books in his arms.

"No, no. I was only curious."

"Oh," he says, sounding relieved. "I didn't even realize I was whistling it. It's...nothing, just a song some friends of mine made up."

"Ah." I nod and slip my cell phone into my purse. "Well, just so you know, I'm going out for lunch in a little while." I glance up at the clock on the wall, a German cuckoo clock that was one of my mother's few personal additions to the store. The yellow-painted bird's about to crow; it's five 'til twelve. "I should be back in an hour or so. Are you up for manning the ship until I get back?"

"Sure. No problem, Courtney."

"Thanks, David."

As he returns to his task, I ease onto the stool and tap my foot, watching the clock's hands tick. But I don't have to wait long. Within the minute, I spot Lare through the tall shop window. She's moving down the sidewalk toward the front door, taking long, measured steps. Her hands are shoved deep into the pockets of her slim cream-colored pants, and her lacy tank top is startlingly white beneath the sharp, chic lines of her black blazer. Her hair is swept over one shoulder, as bright as burnished copper.

She looks distracted, lost in thought; her forehead is creased, her chin bowed down. But then she sees me through the glass, and her expression softens: the worry lines vanish, and her icy blue eyes warm as they seek out mine.

She pulls the door open, bells jangling, as I sling my purse over my shoulder, smiling naturally. Effortlessly. God, I'm practically *skipping* toward her...

When was the last time I was this excited about seeing Mia?

Don't answer that, I command myself, as I pause in front of Lare. "Hi."

"Hi." She tilts her head toward me, matching my smile. Her silver eyes reflect my all-too eager, dog-that's-about-to-go-for-a-walk face. "I'm so glad you were free for lunch," she says quietly, her French accent more pronounced the lower and softer her voice becomes. She lifts her chin, mirrored eyes glinting. "Where would you like to go?" Her full lips turn up into a self-deprecating smile. "I'm afraid I'm not familiar with the restaurants around here. Or, you know, anywhere."

I laugh softly, blushing. Blushing already. Maybe she doesn't notice. Maybe she can't tell how thoroughly and irreversibly smitten I am with her.

And maybe Colette is secretly a Russian spy masquerading as a housecat to gather top-secret foreign intelligence.

Actually, bad metaphor, because *that* might be true...

I stammer, "Okay, restaurants. Um, let me think...." But I can't think. I can't think of a single eatery between Cincinnati and the moon. To conceal my nervousness, I run my hands through my hair, and my traitor fingers—again—get tangled in the strands.

Lare's tired smile softens.

When my hand comes free, she takes it gently, squeezing once, twice.

"Hey, how about that little bistro across the street?" She inclines her head in the direction of Al's Cafe. She hasn't let go of my hand, and my pulse is roaring through me. I feel drunk on her scent, her nearness. I don't want to go to Al's Cafe. I want to take Lare back to my place and—

Focus. You're polite and grateful—remember? Nothing else.

I straighten, clearing my throat and straightening my shoulders, envisioning myself as a Jane Austen heroine wearing one of those empire-waist gowns. "I mean, the"—I make air quotes with my free hand—"*food* is great at Al's Cafe." I offer Lare a weak smile. "If you don't mind penciling food poisoning into your schedule."

"Oh, no..."

"Oh, yes. Azure and I went to Al's once. *Once.* We had to keep the bookstore closed the next day, while we both recovered. That macaroni and cheese... It looks innocent enough. Smells good. But I'm telling you—*lethal.*"

Lare laughs sympathetically. "Okay, so Al's is out of the running."

"Yeah. Oh! How about Cleo's? It's two blocks down the street, and it has this fantastic view of a busy intersection. Live road rage. So *avant-garde.*"

Lare laughs again. "Well, all right. To Cleo's, then." She lets go of my hand to open the door behind her, bowing slightly as she gazes up at me through her long lashes. "After you, *mademoiselle.*"

Heartbeats clacking in my chest like typewriter keys, I duck through the doorway, and Lare follows, letting the door *shush* shut as we step into the sunlight.

The midday heat is brutal, but I hardly notice it; I'm always overheated in Lare's company. The wooden heels of my wedges clonk on the concrete sidewalk as she and I keep pace, side by side. When I look to her, her mouth quirks into a thoughtful but gentle smile. She sighs softly, angling her shoulders forward as her hands disappear into her pants pockets.

"I owe you an explanation, Courtney." Her jaw tenses, and she shifts her silver-blue eyes toward her feet. "I was called in to work last night because of...an unfortunate incident. One that required my immediate attention."

"An incident?"

She nods, almost imperceptibly, and levels me a sober glance. "Yesterday, a colleague of mine, George Morris, was kidnapped from GLT." Her voice is hard, her eyes flashing a dangerous silver. "He's the second GLT employee to vanish recently. So now there's a pattern. Both of the kidnap victims have been human."

I bow my head, taking this information in.

"Give Life Technologies, as you know, concerns itself with blood technology and advancement, so the company is linked undeniably to the welfare of vampires. And there are—as you also know—many, many people who would rather see vampires immolated, exterminated, rather given the opportunity to live happy, open lives."

Shuddering, I think of Drew Yarrow. And I see, in my mind's eye, the photograph of Mia brandishing an anti-vampire sign. "Yeah," I say quietly, "I know."

Lare's nostrils flare. "We have no understanding as to why these humans have been kidnapped, and there aren't any leads—or so the police force claims." She offers me an apologetic shrug. "I don't mean to sound bitter. It's just that... I can't trust them. There have been countless vampire-phobic incidents in this city." Lare trails off, frustrated, biting her lower lip as we round the corner and move past a flower shop called Plantasia. The heady scent of roses wafts around us in the humid air, its sweetness a strange complement to Lare's sour expression.

"Forgive me," she says suddenly.

"Forgive you? For what?" I narrow my brows.

"I've said too much. I shouldn't bother you with my troubles. I only wanted to explain. George is a good man. My friend. He has a family... He doesn't deserve this. Neither does Daniel, the other kidnap victim. I just wish I could figure out what's going on."

"Lare." I stop beside her, and she turns to face me; her eyes are liquid silver, her mouth set in a grim line. I brush my fingertips over her forearm, bared beneath the cuff of her jacket. She's warm to the touch, so soft... Feeling brave, reckless, or some cocktail of both, I glide my fingers down her wrist until I firmly grasp her hand.

"I can't imagine what you're going through. How unsafe you must feel, how...distressed. I'm so sorry." I squeeze her hand as I study her pale, pensive face. "If there's anything I can do to help—to help *you*—just let me know..."

Lare searches my gaze. I see myself in her eyes, a miniature silhouette, and then she blinks, shifts her gaze, and blue replaces the silver. Her lips tug up at the corners. "Do you know what you can do to help me?"

"Just ask," I whisper, squeezing her hand again.

"You can enjoy lunch." She chuckles and gifts me with a brilliant smile that instantly transmutes my knees—and various other parts of my anatomy—into Jell-o.

I lick my lips and lift my brows. "That's all?"

"That's everything. You're outside of my troubles, Courtney. You're...very good for me."

Her smile deepens, and then she nods her head, indicating that we should keep going. Companionably, we begin to walk down the sidewalk again. "And what of your news?" she asks me suddenly, her words subdued.

"News?"

"You said you were going to call me earlier—"

"Oh! God, I'm so scatterbrained today." I slip my phone out of my purse and page through to my folder of saved emails. "A contact of a contact," I tell her, as I scan the email subject lines, "has tracked down a book you might be interested in. He said there are many references to Maximinus in it, along with a whole chapter dedicated solely to his work."

"A whole chapter?" Lare's eyes widen, and her lips part in a wide, expectant smile. I've never seen her smile like this before. All of the sudden, she looks ten years younger, and I can imagine what a beautiful, charming child she must have been. "That's better than I ever hoped for. And you found it so quickly—"

"The only catch," I interrupt, in an attempt to prevent her from getting excited prematurely, "is the price. It's steep. We're talking five figures."

"Hmm." She pauses, turning toward me. "Five figures. But if I pay this price, the book will be mine?"

"Well, yeah," I tell her with a soft smile; she looks adorably happy, as eager as a kid who just found out she's getting a pony for her birthday. "The guy selling the book is a German professor, and everything about him and the book itself seems to check out. There are photos I can show you, and credentials. But..." I draw in a deep breath. "He's asking for $20,000."

Lare doesn't flinch, doesn't even blink. "That's fine. That's fine," she says distractedly, excitedly, removing her hands from her pockets to clasp my fingers. "Courtney, *thank* you. GLT will wire the money to your contact as soon as I pass on the information. I mean, you trust this professor? You think the book is real?"

I nod. "I do."

"Then that's all I need to know. Please get back to him right away, tell him we'll purchase the book. With expedited shipping. Courtney." She bows her head and draws in several long breaths before she lifts her gaze to stare into my eyes. It's a soft stare, and it moves through me like warm water. "I am indebted to you. This could be the answer to—" She stops herself short, setting her mouth in a firm line and lifting her chin. "No. I shouldn't get carried away. Not yet. But I have very high hopes..."

"I'm glad I could help, Lare."

We enter Cleo's, and Lare chooses a small booth in the corner as I type a quick email reply on my phone to Gustav Reigle, communicating Lare's desire to buy his book for his proposed price. I slide into the booth and hit *send* on the message.

"What'll it be, ladies?" My favorite waitress, Charlene, wearing Cleo's standard pink-and-white, vintage-style uniform, asks as she approaches our table.

"I'll have the usual, Char." Charlene is my favorite waitress at Cleo's. Whenever we stop in for dinner, she always tips Azure and I off as to which chef is on duty, and which menu items we should therefore choose—or avoid. Now, Char gives me a wink and a smile before asking Lare what she'd like to order.

"Nothing for me, thanks," Lare says with a soft smile.

If Char sees the silver reflection in Lare's eyes, she doesn't outwardly react to it, just nods and heads toward the back of the diner to bark my order to the afternoon cook. My eyes flick thoughtfully toward the swinging glass entrance. There's a *Vampires welcome here* sign posted on the door, a sign I *must* have seen, subconsciously, every time I walked into the restaurant. But it never really registered—until today. I noticed it when Lare and I came in.

"Nice place." Lare smiles at me across the table, resting her chin on her hand.

"Yeah," I smile back, "it really is. And—hey." I point toward the window at Lare's back. "What did I tell you about that view?"

She laughs as she glances over her shoulder toward the lunch rush traffic, a seemingly endless stream of impatient, hungry nine-to-fivers, swishing past. "Paris would be jealous."

Within minutes, Char brings my grilled cheese-and-tomato sandwich, along with a glass of iced tea. "Here you go, honey. Now, is there anything else I can do for you ladies?"

"I think we're all set. Thanks, Char."

"My pleasure."

I take a sip of the iced tea, and though it's usually something I enjoy—especially on hot days like today—I wrinkle my nose in surprise at the taste. "Wow, Lare," I laugh lightly, placing the glass back on the table. "I have to admit... I think your tea has spoiled me."

"Really?" she asks, lips turning up at the corners.

"Really. I tried that tea packet you gave me, the one you named *Colette*. God, it was...incredible..."

"I'm glad you liked it." Lare's smile widens; she leans forward, hands clasped. My eyes fall to her long fingers and the ring she's wearing on her thumb, a large silver rose. "I was a little worried about the flavors blending well together, but I felt that it needed the extra, hmm, *surprise* that only catnip could provide."

"It was definitely a surprise," I exhale, grinning. "I thought it was the perfect touch. Colette's crazy about catnip." I tear the crusts off of one of the triangles of my sandwich.

"You know," Lare begins with a soft, throaty chuckle, "some people consider catnip to be an aphrodisiac." She leans back in her seat, stares at me with a piercing silver-blue gaze. "Silly, isn't it? But maybe that's why it makes cats lose their senses."

"Maybe." The word is almost a whisper, because my throat closed up when I heard Lare use the word *aphrodisiac*. Her *voice* is an aphrodisiac. Okay, let's be honest—everything about Lare is an aphrodisiac for me. Here we are, spending a simple, casual lunch hour together, and my heart is racing like a jackhammer, my nerves feel as if they've been electrified, and I'm pretty sure my face is the same shade as that ketchup bottle on our table.

I sigh and take a bite of my sandwich.

Lare leans forward again, coppery hair shifting over her shoulders. "If you'd indulge me, Courtney, I do need a taste tester for another tea blend," she says, her head tilted to one side, her mouth slanting encouragingly. "It's brand-new—as of this morning, in fact. Making it helped relax me when I got home from..." Her expression darkens as she trails off, shaking her head. She gazes down at the tabletop, unseeing, for a handful of heartbeats. Then her lips part, and she says, simply, "I call it Carmilla."

"Carmilla," I repeat, with a nostalgic smile. I read *Carmilla* in college for my Gothic Lit class with Professor Dugal. The little book left a lasting impression on me, and no wonder: it was the only time I had a class assignment that involved reading a novel with a lesbian main character.

And a *vampire* lesbian main character, to boot.

"I'd love to taste-test your tea," I say.

"Well, good, because I would love to have you taste-test my tea."

And the wheels in my brain begin to squeak, and squeal, and finally, with one last rusty grunt, turn.

So, this is a tea blend named Carmilla. And Lare made another blend named Colette. And yet another she called Oscar Wilde. There's an obvious literary theme here, and the teas taste amazing, unlike anything I've ever tried before...

Hmm.

Yeah...

Okay, it's happening.

141

I'm starting to get one of my Wild Ideas.

Normally, I get my Wild Ideas when Azure is there to talk me down, to tell me that my whim is either outrageous (and totally doable) or outrageous (and totally *not* doable). She's the one who, gently but firmly, persuaded me to resist the urge to get that buzz cut back in college, and that tattoo of my sophomore year girlfriend's name inked on my shoulder—in Comic Sans font, no less.

She's the one who, not so gently and *very* firmly, persuaded me *not* to date Mia Foster. Advice which I soundly ignored but which, in retrospect, may have had more wisdom in it than I realized at the time.

Anyway, Azure isn't here right now, and Lare *is*, so....

I draw in a deep breath.

"Lare," I begin, swirling the straw in my glass so that the ice cubes rattle.

"Courtney." She gives me a sideways smile, one eyebrow raised.

"Okay, feel free to say no, and I'm probably out of line for suggesting this, but..." I pause nervously before the question, of its own accord, just kind of spills out of my mouth: "Would you ever consider *selling* your teas...at a bookstore, perhaps?"

"Mm." Lare looks thoughtful, leaning back in the booth. "A bookstore..." She bites her lower lip, serious, considering—but then, within moments, that sexy smile breaks out over her face again, and her eyes flash at me like silver moonbeams. "Well, you know, it would have to be a really *fantastic* bookstore." She inclines her head of red waves toward me with a teasing smirk. "Owned by my really fantastic next-door neighbor."

Excitement rushes through me. I'm *so* excited that I almost spill my tea, and I only spare a millisecond to inwardly revel over the *really fantastic* compliment. "You'd be interested in doing it? Seriously? Because it's as if my store were made for this purpose! There's an old counter in the back of the shop—my dad used to dream of serving customers coffee and donuts, but he never had the chance to make that dream happen before he died. If I did some research, got the proper permits, maybe we could set up a tea bar, some cafe tables..." I trail off; I feel like I'm short-circuiting. I press the backs of my hands to my hot cheeks. "Sorry. I'm getting carried away here."

"No, no." Lare smiles, her eyes soft and blue and fond. Her lips quirk up subtly as she gazes at me. "I like seeing you get...carried away."

"Oh... Um. Thanks."

She watches me for a moment longer, still smiling that small, mysterious, Mona Lisa smile. And then she drums her fingers on the table and nods decisively. "Let's do this."

"Are you sure?"

"*Oui.* Very sure." She breathes out, and her gaze slides to my lips—brazenly, teasing me. When her eyes flick back up to meet mine, they're as clear and blue as the summer sky. "I'll put together some packets of tea to sell and some to brew. I could probably get them to you next week. Well, barring any further incidents at work." For a heartbeat, pain flickers over her face, but it's gone as quickly as it appeared, and she reaches across the table, extending her hand to me.

I assume that she wants to shake on our new, unexpected venture, but when my hand slides into Lare's, her fingers curl and lift my hand toward her mouth. She leans down, brushing her warm lips against the backs of my knuckles.

"I'm delighted to have such a lovely business partner," she whispers against my skin.

Then, with a soft, slanting smile, she lets go of my hand.

Some distant, observant part of me is aware that my eyes have opened wide and that my lips have suggestively parted. And I can't... No, I *can't* think about what just happened—about Lare's mouth, shaping words for me, kissing me... *Don't think about it.* I'll stop functioning entirely if I do. I'll say things, do things, that I can't say or do, not as a woman in a committed relationship.

So, instead, I focus on the *non*-sexual thrills pinging through my body over the fact that we're going to create a tea bar at Banks' Books. I haven't felt this excited about a project—or the shop—in a long time. I pick up my sandwich and take a big, messy, satisfying bite.

"My dad would love this idea," I think out loud, as I wipe my mouth with a paper napkin. "I mean, he was a coffee drinker—black coffee, nothing fancy—and he never drank tea. But the reason he bought that counter was because he wanted to introduce a way for our customers to relax in the store, to spend some time there, feel comfortable, read, escape their busy lives." I take another bite pensively and then sip at my iced tea. "He always used to tell me that he wanted the store to be more than a store. He wanted it to feel like a home away from home. That's how it always felt for him." I smile softly. "And for me. It still feels that way."

"It's a special place. I knew it the moment I stepped through the door."

I fall into Lare's cool, silver-blue eyes. She's leaning back in the booth, watching me with an easy smile. "Thank you. This... This really means a lot to me. And it'll get the word out about your teas—everyone will be talking about them once they give them a try. And who knows? Maybe maybe this will breathe some life back into my gasping little store."

Lare chuckles softly, glancing down at her hands in her lap.

Suddenly self-conscious, I ask her, "What?"

"Oh, nothing. It's just... You're beautiful when you're like this. So full of...hope." She smiles at me, the soft points of her teeth visible between her lips.

I blush, stare down at my now-empty plate, as I think — and hate myself for thinking — about how those teeth, that mouth, would feel against my mouth —

"I'm afraid we'll have to continue this discussion later."

I look up, surprised, and Lare gestures to the clock on the diner wall. She rises quickly, gracefully, with an apologetic smile. "I must get back to the lab, but we'll talk very soon, yes?" She pulls a slim wallet out of her back pocket and presses a ten dollar bill to the table.

"No, you don't have to—"

"My treat," she insists. Her gaze is complicated, intense. Seeing the reflection of myself in her silvered eyes makes me feel strange, small, but a little euphoric, as if some part of me already belongs to her, is part of her.

Well, we are more than next-door neighbors now. We're business partners. And being business partners involves an inordinate amount of trust. It's a definite level-up, as far as relationships go. Granted, it isn't exactly the sort of relationship I want—or daydream about—with Lare, but it'll be a great step for both of us. I know it will.

Because Lare was right: I am full of hope.

"Thank you." I smile up at her awkwardly. I feel like a girl on a first date, a date that just went surprisingly well, and that's really, really not how I should be feeling right now. "I mean, for everything. I'll call you with the details for wiring your payment for that book. And...yeah. We'll talk soon."

"*Au revoir*, Courtney." Lare touches her fingertips to the back of my hand in an oddly intimate gesture. Then she turns and walks out the door. Through the diner window, I watch her move down the street, admiring the lyricism of her limbs, the surety of her every step.

When I get back to the shop, I dig through a pile of estate sale acquisitions that I haven't cataloged yet. And there it is, just like I remembered it—a gold-gilt copy of *Carmilla* bound in burgundy leather.

Perched on my stool, I lose myself in the story's dark passages until closing time.

Apparently, my parents were incapable of producing a conventional daughter. There's me, the book-devouring lesbian. And then there's my younger sister Sharon—the artist goth who lives in a converted firehouse downtown.

She shares the firehouse with her boyfriend Marcus and an ever-changing group of eccentric roommates. The decor of the place is industrial, exposed ducts and brickwork, and Sharon's paintings—of cemeteries, mostly—cover the unpainted walls. The gloomy decor fits, Sharon's always joking, because many of her roommates, including her boyfriend, are vampires.

I was so flustered and overstimulated after having lunch with Lare that I nearly forgot Sharon had invited me to join her for dinner tonight. I had to speed all the way from the bookshop. Of course, "speeding," in Colonel Mustard's automotive dictionary, is defined as, "stalling out in three intersections and refusing to accelerate above thirty miles per hour."

But, hey, I made it in one piece, and only half an hour late.

When I knock on the broad front door and Sharon ushers me inside, I notice a large group of people in the common area, playing video games on a huge pull-down projector screen and eating pizza.

Well, the humans are eating pizza.

Sharon squeezes me in a tight hug with an exuberant, "You're late! But we saved you some 'za." She grabs one of the boxes of pizza and pulls me up the wide antique stairs, original to the firehouse, and heads toward the bedroom she shares with Marcus. "How are things at the shop?" Sharon asks, holding the door open for me.

"Okay. No, they're good...and getting better." I walk into the bedroom, taking in the black walls, the Dumpster-dived furnishings, the big zombie painting hanging above the queen-sized bed—which, of course, is draped in black velvet.

I smile to myself as I remember how my sister, when she was in elementary school, used to insist on wearing dresses every day—*pink* dresses, the puffier the better, with layers with tulle stuffed under wide, watermelon-colored princess skirts. With her blonde curls and pretty mannerisms, she was on the fast-track to becoming a princess or a prima ballerina when she grew up.

But, well...times have changed.

I watch my sister as she sets the pizza box on the bed and turns toward me with a triumphant smile. Her hair—once more yellow than mine—is now dyed jet black and chopped in a punk, A-line cut. Adult Sharon wouldn't be caught *dead* in anything pink; she wears all black, head to toe, and the more metal, the better. I've lost track of how many piercings she has.

The entrepreneurial gene that runs rampant in our family manifested in her, too, because Sharon has never worked a "traditional" job. She scraped along until she made it, and made it big, selling her gothic artwork on Etsy for a living.

"So," she says, head tilted to the side as she raises a black-penciled brow, needling me with her emerald green gaze. "What's *up*?"

"Oh, you know..." I bite my lip thoughtfully. I'm not really prepared to spill any details about Lare yet. I'm still feeling overwhelmed and speechless about the whole *business partners* thing. "Just...the usual. Um... What's going on with you?" We both sit down on the edge of the bed and take slices out of the box of pizza, making twin sounds of contentment as we relish the gooey cheese.

"Well, I'm *ridiculously* stoked about the music festival tomorrow night," says Sharon, around another huge bite. "Marcus is going with me, as are all of the roomies. We picked up our tickets the minute they went on sale." She pinches a long string of cheese stretched between her mouth and the slice and gobbles it up with a satisfied smile, just like she used to when we were kids. "I've been planning my outfit for weeks. I got these *sickening* fishnet arm warmers from the alternative arts and crafts fair, hand-crocheted. I can't wait to show them to you." She pauses, lips pursed, and gives me a sidelong glance. "What are *you* wearing?"

I shrug, and immediately Sharon casts her

eyes to the black-painted ceiling, despairing over her big sister's nonexistent fashion sense.

"Come on. This event isn't exactly...my *scene*. I mean, I don't have *any* fishnet arm warmers, hand-crocheted or otherwise," I tease her.

But Sharon is already standing up, her half-eaten slice flung to the lid of the open pizza box. She opens her closet doors with a dramatic sweep of her arms and pulls a series of very black clothes off of very black hangers. Then she wordlessly tosses the dark bundle at me.

"Sharon. This really..." I hold up a short black skirt, a zippered black tank top and a pair of black fishnet tights. "...isn't me."

"It is a truth universally acknowledged that music festivals provide a prime opportunity to show off, to dress *up*," Sharon tells me with a wheedling smile.

"No fair, bringing a literary reference into this. You know that's my weakness."

"Seriously, Court, just give the outfit a shot! You can wear boring bookstore clothes if you want to, but you'll stand out like a sore...librarian."

"Hey, I resemble that remark," I laugh, folding the clothes neatly before grabbing another slice of pizza. "God, this is so good."

"Food of the gods." She falls back onto the bed beside me with an *oof*.

From the common room downstairs,

there's a sudden, muffled outbreak of laughter.

"It seems like there are more people here than usual. Have you signed on some new roommates?" I ask curiously.

Sharon shakes her head, picking up her discarded piece of pizza. "No, most of the people downstairs are part of VampWatch. You know, the Vampire Neighborhood Watch. Remember? I mentioned them to you before."

I nod, thinking as I chew. "Yeah, I remember." According to Sharon, VampWatch is the most outspoken group of pro-vampire advocates in Cincinnati. She and Marcus are active members.

"Well, anyway, we just had a meeting, and it got pretty intense. So now everyone's chilling, playing video games and goofing around to take the edge off."

I stiffen slightly. "Oh? What was the meeting about?"

"Working out a plan to combat Drew Yarrow," my sister mutters, her eyes green slits, "and her *disgusting* hate group, SANG."

"Right. That's what I was afraid you were going to say..."

"What?" Sharon pauses mid-bite to blink at me, confused. "What do you mean, that's what—"

"Look." I sigh for a long moment. My sister continues to stare at me as if I've grown a second head. Frowning, I drop my pizza slice into the box; I've suddenly lost my appetite. "I've got something to tell you."

Sharon leans toward me, brow furrowed. "What's wrong, Court?" she asks gently.

I fret at the edge of the paper napkin in my lap, feeling the pain that I've purposefully pushed down, ignored, well up inside of my chest, my throat. I straighten my spine, gaze mournfully into my sister's shining eyes. "I think Mia is involved with Drew."

"Drew." Sharon shakes her head, as if waiting for me to say something more. Then understanding dawns over her face, and she shakes her head harder. "No. You mean... No. Drew...*Yarrow*? *That* Drew?"

"Yeah. That Drew."

Sharon gapes.

"I mean, I don't know for *certain* if they're having an affair," I say, raking a hand back through my tangles with a heavy sigh. "Mia has been, I don't know, *interviewing* Drew or something. Following her around to get a story for her paper. Or so she's told me. But I saw this picture of them together, a photo of Mia demonstrating with SANG..." I trail off. My eyes are stinging, and I sag on the bed, sunken down by the weight of the matter. "I just don't know who she is anymore."

"Oh, Court." Sharon places a hand on my shoulder and squeezes.

I smile at her weakly. "It's okay. Really.

I mean, it hurts to realize you've misjudged someone so much, but...the truth of the matter is that I want to break up with Mia. I've wanted to for a while. There's always been something *missing* in our relationship, you know?"

Sharon watches me sympathetically.

I breathe out. "When I told Mia that I thought we should go our separate ways, though, she asked for another chance. And...I couldn't deny her that. She said she was sorry. She seemed sincere. But..." I swallow and bite my lip.

"But..." my sister prompts me, staring very intently at my face.

I stop tearing the napkin and draw in another deep gulp of air. "*But* the thing is," I say softly, quietly, "I'm attracted to someone else."

My sister begins to smile, but, to her credit, she forcibly flattens her mouth, trying to maintain the straightest expression possible. She holds her tongue, simply raises her eyebrows and waits for me to go on.

"I'm attracted," I tell her, knowing that my next words are going to overwhelm her oh-so-fake appearance of composure, "to the vampire who moved in next door—"

Sharon squeals, launching herself forward and wrapping her arms tightly around my neck. "Didn't I *tell* you that Mia was bad news from the moment I met her?" She sits back, her black-painted fingernails curled around my shoulders. "I mean, God, she's *such* a wet mop. Point her in the direction of a pretty woman, and she'll follow that tail like a bloodhound on a scent—" She makes a little gasp and covers her mouth with her hand. "God, I'm sorry. Too soon. Now's not the time, I know."

She gives me another quick hug before peering keenly into my eyes. "Seriously, though, I need *details*. A *vampire?* I feel it fair to warn you, sis," she begins with a cheeky smile, "that once you go fangs, you never go—"

"God, Sharon, it's not like that," I tell her miserably, burying my face in my hands. I can feel the all-too-familiar blush creeping over my cheeks.

"*Details*, Courtney. You can't drop a bombshell like *I'm attracted to a vampire* and then just leave me hanging."

"I won't. Calm down."

"Inquiring minds want to know—"

"*Okay*," I begin, sighing as I try to piece together a chain of inarticulate emotions. How do I describe Lare? How do I explain how her voice, her eyes, her nearness affects me?

I *can't*. Not to my little sister. Not now. It's all too new, too soft and unformed. Too raw.

I decide to stick to the facts: "Her name is Lare—Valeria—and she's a scientist at Give Life Technologies."

"A *scientist* vampire," Sharon informs me

helpfully, holding up her index finger, "is super hot."

I roll my eyes at her—even as I silently agree. "Um, she has a Saint Bernard. She's possibly French. And...that's about all I have to tell you." I tug at an errant knot in my hair. "It's just a crush. I'd never cheat on Mia," I say firmly.

"Of course not. I never thought you would." Sharon arches one brow as she watches me carefully. "I know you better than that."

"Thanks."

She shrugs, then crosses her legs on the bed with a wicked smile. "I can't lie, though. I'm really happy that you're thinking of splitting up with Mia. She's been bad news from the start, you know? I was shocked when you introduced me to her. She's so...flighty. She never struck me as the type of person Courtney Banks, Perfectionist, could fall in love with."

My lips part, and we both stare at one another for a long moment.

"What? What did I say?" Sharon asks nervously. "You look sick... Was it the pizza? Do you need to throw up?"

Well, while my soul is already bare...

"Sharon," I start, voice hushed, my mouth as dry as ash. "I don't even know if I believe in love. I mean...*love* love. Falling in love, true love, soul mates... That kind of stuff."

My sister watches me, unblinking—

stunned or bored, it's hard to tell.

I sigh. "You were right there with me, Share," I tell her hoarsely, flicking my gaze to my hands in my lap. "Our parents fought like cats and dogs. No," I reconsider, twisting my mouth to one side, "they fought like *rabid* cats and dogs. They fought about *everything*: the bookstore, us. They fought about *dinner*. They were the most incompatible people in the world, and that's what I see over and over again. I see incompatible people coming together and just...hurting each other. It's this vicious cycle that no one else seems to notice."

Sharon remains still and quiet as I stand up, tossing my torn napkin into her silver, skull-embossed trashcan. I smooth my hands over my skirt, shaking my head as I turn back to her. My throat is tight. "You know I enjoy reading love stories. Like *Jane Eyre*. It's my favorite book. But, I mean, I love reading ghost stories, too — and that doesn't mean I believe in ghosts. I've been in enough relationships to wonder," I breathe, "if maybe love is only a work of fiction, after all."

Sharon opens her mouth, is about to say something, but then there's a soft rap at the partially shut bedroom door.

"Hey, I just wanted to see how you guys are doing. Can I come in, or are you ladies dishing about the latest *RuPaul's Drag Race*? If you are — *spoilers!* 'Cause I haven't seen the episode yet." Marcus grins companionably, peering around the edge of the door.

Sharon and I laugh, grateful for the break in the tension. Then, like a black leather-clad gazelle, Sharon leaps from the bed and springs to the door, reaching out for her boyfriend's hand. "Come on in, snooper."

"Sorry." Marcus ducks into the room with an apologetic shrug, a dimpled smile adorning his boyishly handsome face. He gathers Sharon into his arms, and the intimate act comes so naturally, as if Sharon is an extension of his own body. He leans down and kisses my sister deeply but somehow softly; she sighs against him.

As a couple, they've never been shy about public displays of affection.

And, yeah, the love Marcus and Sharon share is unquestioningly real. They've been together for five years and just got engaged last spring—though they claim that they knew, from their very first date, that they were destined to marry one another. They've been saving up for the whole length of their relationship to finance the nuptials of their gothic dreams: a destination wedding in—where else?—Transylvania. They intend to promise their undying love in the place that—mythically, at least—the undead call home.

After smacking lips in another passionate kiss, Marcus and Sharon draw apart, and Sharon taps his chin with her finger, says, "We'll be right down, okay?"

Marcus nods, baring his vampire teeth as he grins at me. "No rush. Come on down when you're done gabbing, and we can all watch the episode together. The VampWatch crew's gone home, so now it's just me and the roomies playing Mario Kart." He offers us a small salute before turning on his heel to disappear down the hallway.

Sharon pushes the door closed; then she stretches out her arm to tug at my hand. "Look, Court," she tells me gently, squeezing my fingers. "Think about what Dad always used to tell us when we came to him for advice. You remember, right?"

My throat tightens, but I nod, whisper, "*If you were reading the story of your life, what would you want you – the heroine – to do right now?*"

Sharon and I stare at one another for a long moment as my pulse begins to accelerate. The thing is, before I even spoke those words—a well-worn litany that formed on my lips as easily as the Pledge of Allegiance—I knew my answer. I could never bring myself to say it out loud, but it's there. And it's so obvious, it hurts.

Even if nothing ever happens between myself and Lare, my relationship with Mia has been in its death throes for weeks, if not months. And it's harmful to both of us to be half of a failing relationship. We're not right for each other. I thought I was in love with her—or deluded myself into thinking that I was, that I must be. But I wasn't.

I'm not.

Mia deserves someone who can love her for who she is, for everything that she is, with an unwavering constancy. An unshakable certainty.

I'm not that person. I can't do that for her. And I don't think she can do that for me.

It's over.

I gasp, caving inward, and am only vaguely aware of Sharon's arms wrapped around me. I feel as if I've just been thwacked in the chest with one of those anvils that always appear in old-school cartoons.

But even as the resolve hardens inside of me to break up with Mia *tonight*, I remember the hurt look on her face when I attempted to break up with her a couple of days ago, how the tears stood shining in her eyes...

God, I can't handle that expression again, not yet.

"Just...think about it," says Sharon quietly, watching me.

I shake my head, suddenly exhausted. "Hey, could you tell Marcus that I'm sorry I can't—that it's just been..." With a heavy sigh, I stand up and lean against the ornate dresser. Its surface is decorated with framed photographs of Sharon and Marcus—laughing, kissing, sharing a candy apple at the state fair. I stare at the pictures dully. "I think I'm going to go home, go to bed early. I'm just...drained."

Sharon springs up beside me and gives me a tight hug. "Don't forget these." She shoves the pile of black clothes into my arms.

Outside of the old fire station, a humid summer rain is beginning to fall in large, heavy drops. I run toward my car, but the deluge soaks me through before I reach it.

Through my damp, dripping lashes, the whole world looks as if it's been painted watercolor gray.

Chapter Six: Love and Hate

My fantasy of escaping to the misty moors of *Jane Eyre* while soaking in a hot, sudsy bubble bath evaporates the moment that I pull into my driveway.

I lean forward over the wheel, watching my house's blurry silhouette through the raindrops splattering on the windshield.

Something feels...wrong.

Maybe I'm just projecting, or absorbing the gloomy atmosphere. Dark storm clouds are hanging over the edge of the horizon, and the rain is falling silently, steadily. With an unaccountable dread, I slump out of Colonel Mustard and shut the car door. It thuds dully, and the rain thuds dully, too, on the top of my head: *thud, thud, thud.* My feet feel heavier and heavier with each step, as if they're urging me to stop, turn around, go back...

Just as I'm putting my key into the lock, the front door of my house opens beneath my hand.

And Mia's standing on the other side.

I freeze.

"Mia."

I wouldn't be more shocked if a ghost

suddenly materialized before me. Mia is the last person I expected to see right here, right now. The last person I wanted to see, given my state of mind.

She stares at me with wide, dark eyes surrounded by darker circles. "Hi," she says shortly, stepping back and gesturing toward the room behind her. "Come on in."

"What are you doing here?" My voice is icier than I intended, icier than I feel. "I mean, your car isn't in the driveway. How did you—" I begin, but Mia shakes her head, moves further back into the shadows of the house.

She looks agitated, haunted. Her long brown hair is drawn up into a messy bun. She's usually neat, even vain about her physical appearance. And I've never seen her wear a collared, button-down shirt before. This one is oversize, and the sleeves are rolled up to her elbows. The sight reminds me of those girls in high school who strutted through the hallways wearing their boyfriends' too-big varsity jackets.

I draw in a deep breath, and my stomach churns inside of me as I wonder—how can I help but wonder?—if the shirt Mia is wearing belongs to Drew Yarrow.

She doesn't kiss me, greet me. Doesn't speak at all. Impatient, she grabs my arm, and, instead of pulling me into the house, she yanks me back outside, beneath the silvery, pouring rain.

And her gaze is pointed very, well, *pointedly* toward Lare's house.

Oh, God...

I wrap my arms around my middle and bow my head, bracing myself. Raindrops slide over the bridge of my nose and drip from the tip of it, plinking softly to the ground below. Cold water streams over my lowered lids.

"Do you know who's living next door to you?" Mia asks, voice knife sharp. She's staring at me now, her eyes wide, wild, and growing wider and wilder as she waits for me to answer.

I stand my ground, lift my chin, my own words colder than the iceberg that sank the *Titanic,* and with the same cutting edge. "Yes. I know Valeria Máille. She's a customer of mine—"

"A *customer?*"

Okay, I expected Mia to be pissed—given her new anti-vampire lifestyle.

But I didn't expect her to *explode*.

"Are you *kidding* me, Courtney?" she snarls, her narrow face paling as her lips draw back to reveal a row of very white, very human teeth. "She's a *monster,* and you're saying she bought *books* from you, that you let her come into your *shop*? How could you allow that *thing* to get anywhere near you and your employees?"

As I gape at her in horror, stunned to silence, her face smooths. The lines on her forehead are gone; the frown is replaced with a neutral curve. This instant calm seems even more unsettling than her angry outburst. I take a step back.

"Listen to me, Courtney." Her tone is low, even, and sinister. I've never heard Mia speak this way before, or look this way — so tense, as if she's on the verge of violence. "You can't associate with her anymore. You *can't*. In any way. It's as simple as that," she says firmly, darkly, her eyes flashing with an unfamiliar light. "You can't be linked to the vampire agenda."

I remain still, wordless, for several seconds. The ground feels as if it's tilting beneath my feet, as if it might give way at any moment. I press fingers to my temple and force out, "Did you honestly just say *vampire agenda?*"

My body has gone cold. Disbelieving, I grit my teeth together, stare hard into her unflinching eyes. "Tell me, Mia," I say, unable to keep the bitterness out of my voice, "are those Drew's *exact* words, or did you do a little creative revision of your own?"

Mia snarls again — actually *snarls* — and moves nearer, her hands curling into fists at her sides. We stand before one another, facing off, and I can't think, can't react, can't do anything but marvel over this change, this *metamorphosis*. Mia is acting like a completely different person, like a junkie in need of a fix.

I don't know who she is. She's a stranger.

My girlfriend has become a stranger to me.

My mind whirls and my heart stutters in my chest, but I refuse to back down. I won't look away. And, finally, Mia relents, because that's what Mia does. Her yielding gives me a small flare of hope—not for our relationship but for Mia's well-being. A portion of the old Mia is still inside of her, though Drew has worked something supernatural, reinventing her in such a short amount of time...

I watch mutely as Mia turns on her heel and, with an exaggerated sigh, marches back into my house. I follow her to my kitchen, where she grabs her purse off of the counter and stomps toward me with a huff.

"We're done," Mia snaps, inches away from my face. Then, without another word, she runs back outside.

"Wait—" Groaning in frustration, I follow her into the rain again. The storm is at its peak, with wind rattling through the gutters. "Mia—"

"Look, I didn't come here to argue. I just wanted to give you these." She digs around in her purse for a moment; then she pulls out a large stack of papers. Glossy brochures. "I thought you could put them out with the free newspapers in your bookstore."

I almost take the stack from her, simply to put an end to this painful encounter, but then I

167

realize what the brochures are, and my arm recoils: SANG fliers. She's shoving *SANG* fliers at me, and in clear view of Lare's house.

The enemy is very real and all around us is printed in bold typeface on the front of the fliers, along with a purposefully insulting photograph of a man wearing white face paint. Blood dribbles over his chin from comically oversized fangs.

I can't hide my disgust. Still, Mia wags the brochures at me, urging me to take them, despite the fact that they're now floppy and soaked.

I try to keep my voice steady as I say, in a clear, tight voice, "I will *never* distribute SANG literature in my bookstore. SANG is a hate group. Mia, I think you've been brainwashed—"

"Brainwashed?" She stares at me with saucer-wide eyes, deeply startled, as if I've just announced the impossible, that I'm from the planet Neptune, or that I've suddenly realized I'm straight. "They haven't *brainwashed* me," she says, with a small laugh of conviction. "God, if anything, they've opened my eyes!" Her cheeks are pale, and her hair is drenched. I notice now, too, that she appears as if she's lost some weight. She looks like a ghost of her former self. "Courtney, *Billy* was killed by a vampire. You *know* that."

"Billy..." I breathe out.

Billy was Mia's brother. Two years ago, he

walked into a convenience store at the wrong time, during a robbery, and he was shot and killed by a perpetrator who turned out to be a vampire.

I inhale and exhale several times, gathering my thoughts and softening my tone. "Mia, your brother was killed by a *criminal*. I'm sorry for your loss. You know I am. I know you and Billy were close. But isn't it very obvious to you that you can't blame *all* vampires for the actions of a single one? You can't be this narrow-minded."

I squeeze my eyes shut as Mia's face begins to crumple. I want to reach for her, comfort her, but she feels so far away from me, worlds away.

"Mia," I continue quietly, "I...I'm sorry Billy died. But you have to realize that the vampire who killed him doesn't represent every vampire, or any vampire. He and he alone was responsible for his actions."

A tear streaks down Mia's face, disappearing in the rain, as she sighs, draws back her shoulders, and curtly nods her head. "Drew told me you would say that," she whispers, eyes shining with a gleam that makes me, reflexively, shiver. "Last night, when she and I were...*talking*—"

I wince at her emphasis of the word.

"—she told me that you wouldn't understand. That I shouldn't even try to explain anything to you. But I'm not going to give up, Courtney," says Mia, her eyes still fervent, afire. "I want you to see the *truth*. I want us to be together in this. Because it's right, Courtney. I swear to you, it is." She claims my hand with her cold, clammy fingers, but I slip free from her and draw away.

"No." My heart aches in time with the thunderclap cracking overhead. "We will never agree about this."

"But—"

"No, Mia."

She stares at me through the rain, her lips softly parted, her gaze dimming as their hopeful shine, moment by moment, fades.

There's nothing left for either of us to say.

I gulp down a breath of cold air, turn around slowly, and walking back toward my house.

I don't expect her to call out for me.

And she doesn't.

Sodden and miserable, I walk through the front door, shutting it and locking it behind me.

There's the sound of a car swishing up to the curb a few minutes later, and when I draw back the curtain to look out through the window, Mia is gone.

It's been a slow week. And a difficult one.

I haven't heard from Mia since our awful conversation in the rain. I keep replaying the scene, hearing her insist upon a "vampire agenda" while pointing at the house next door like the judge probably pointed at the unfairly accused women of Salem.

I can't bring myself to call Mia after what happened.

We left things on such bad terms, and at an impasse.

That second chance she asked of me seems to have fizzled out, officially expired.

God, I hate loose ends. I hate doors left open to invite in more upset and pain. I have to contact her. I have to officially break up with her. But when is the right time? And how can I drum up the fortitude to do it when my heart is already shattered?

Finally, it's Friday morning, and I've never been more grateful for the end of the workweek in my life.

I stand behind the counter in the shop, taking a sip from my to-go coffee cup as I juggle my cell, calling up Mia's number and then chickening out—*again*—before I can force myself to press *send*.

I wince a little as hot liquid burns my mouth; the phone clatters out of my hand, sliding onto a pile of mail. At the same moment, the store telephone begins to ring. For a nerve-wracking moment, I think it must be Mia calling.

But then David ducks his head out of the back office doorway. "Courtney, there's someone named Gustav on the phone for you." He holds up the cordless. "Didn't say what he was calling about."

I put down my coffee and wave my hand in front of my mouth, eyes watering, as I accept the receiver from him. "Thanks, David," I say around my burnt tongue, and then I blink a dozen times and clear my throat.

"Hello? Professor?" I say into the phone.

"Ms. Banks?" His accent is thick, German, and his voice is deep. "Apologies for my delayed response, but I would be very pleased to send that book to you. You will wire me the money, yes?"

"Yes! Yes, I will. Thank you. Um..." I hop onto my stool and open up the laptop. "Did you send me the information I need to wire payment to you?"

"It is coming to your email, even as we speak," he says. I can hear the smile in his voice. "I was very...interested as to why your client would desire such a book, Ms. Banks, I must confess." He *harrumphs* for a moment. "I am an expert on alchemical texts, you see, and Maximinus' work is not well known, though it was revolutionary for his time. And, quite frankly, still is."

I log in to my email account and scan for the message from Gustav. It's there, right between an email from Azure about the concert and a spam email alerting me to the presence of *sexy naughty hot single local guys.*

"He was a revolutionary? How so?" I ask absentmindedly, as I scribble notes onto a legal pad.

"Well, Maximinus was attempting to create a substance that looked, behaved, and even *tasted* like blood—without using animal or human materials."

I drop my pen, heart pounding.

A *blood* substitute...

"Hold on a second." I swallow and shift the phone to my other ear. "You mean... This guy was trying to *make* blood that wasn't actually blood?"

"Simply put, yes," says Gustav, with an almost audible shrug. "Or so his biographers claim. There are detailed descriptions in the book, actually, about his scientific methods. Apparently, he had some success in his endeavor, but no one, to my knowledge, has attempted his experiments since."

I listen, rapt, my mind racing. The successful creation of synthetic blood would... Well, it would change the world. On top of revolutionizing the medical industry, it would rewrite the futures of human- *and* vampirekind.

My arms are covered in goosebumps. I'm playing the middleman to history here. My voice sounds excited, wired, when I say, "I'll get back to my client right away with the information you sent me. I should expect the wire transfer to occur today. She—my client—is very eager to get this book in her hands, so I hope that you'll be able to ship it quickly."

"Wonderful! Wonderful. I will do this." Gustav chuckles softly. "It was a pleasure, Ms. Banks. A pleasure."

And, just like that, the line goes dead.

I'm too stunned for extended small talk right now, anyway.

I grip the counter, stare down at the wire transfer details I scribbled onto the notepad.

If Lare could do this, if she could really *do* this impossible thing...

Vampires wouldn't have to drink real blood anymore. The taboo would be irrelevant, eradicated. And if it wasn't real blood they were drinking...well, then, wouldn't vampires be just like us? Living creatures who must ingest specific nutrients to survive?

The senseless hatred would have to stop, or lessen significantly, as the differences between us decreased. Wouldn't it?

I shake my head, pick up my cell phone and the legal pad, angling toward the back office. David is done filing in there and is now whistling somewhere between the shelves of the shop.

I need to speak with Lare right away.

I dial her number, excited about the book

but also—truthfully—excited for this excuse to speak with her again.

We haven't talked since our lunch date. She's busy with her work at the lab, and she is, understandably, stressed out over the kidnappings. As much as I've longed to call her, and see her, I've resisted the urge to initiate contact, because I don't want to further complicate her life by entangling her in *my* complicated life.

And honestly? I was reluctant to talk to her again before I'd broken up with Mia.

There's just...something about Lare. And something about *me* when I'm around Lare. I wanted to have a clear conscience the next time we spoke—no guilt, no self-imposed restrictions...

But, unfortunately, I'm a shaking-in-my-boots *coward* and am still, technically, in a relationship with Mia.

Lare answers on the second ring.

"Courtney." Her voice is tired but warm. I can hear her smiling against the phone. "How are you?"

I smile, too, feeling a hot rush move through my limbs and flush my cheeks. "I'm doing well," I tell her. *I'm doing well* now, I think. "Listen, Gustav just called me. Finally. I have the wire transfer information—"

"Oh, *magnifique*," she says, and then she takes down the details as I relay them, but she seems distant, distracted. I can hear background voices on her end of the line, as if there are multiple people in the room with her. Maybe I interrupted her during a meeting. After Lare takes down the final number from me, she says quickly, "Just one moment, please."

More muffled talking while I wait, tapping my pen on the legal pad anxiously.

"Courtney?" says Lare at last. Her voice sounds different now, more relaxed, open. And the other voices are gone. "Are you still there?"

"I'm here."

"Sorry. I had to move to a different room. I am really so glad that you called." Her tone is soft, velvety, but then she sighs—a weary sigh, as if she's bone-deep exhausted. "It has been a terrible week, *ma belle*. So, so terrible."

Ma belle. My high school French is rusty, but I can guess at her meaning; a delicious shiver courses through my veins.

Focus, Courtney.

I narrow my brows and shake my head. "What's happened? What's wrong? Are you okay?"

"Another of my co-workers has gone missing," she tells me tiredly. "That makes three. And everyone at GLT is afraid they will be next."

"Oh, my God," I whisper. "I'm so sorry." My stomach twists as I bite my lip. "Do you think you're in danger?"

"At this point," says Lare, her voice quiet, subdued, "the targeted victims have been human. But the circumstances are odd. No ransoms have been requested—which makes it all the more...puzzling. I am friends with the latest victim's wife, so I'm about to leave work to spend the day with her, to try to console her, if I can."

"God, Lare..." My lungs feel as if they're being pinched; every breath takes a concerted effort. I wish I had words of comfort to offer. I wish I could think of some way to help. I can't imagine what Lare and her co-workers must be going through. I am certain that, if the employees at Banks' Books started disappearing, I would be a wreck, a disaster.

I would be useless and petrified with fear.

The fact that Lare is still functioning astounds me.

Admittedly, there isn't anything about Lare that *fails* to astound me...

"On an unrelated note," she begins, a small ray of brightness edging her tone, "I would... I would like to see you tonight, if you're available."

Open-mouthed, I pause, computing her carefully chosen words: *I would like to see you tonight, if you're available.*

Lare wants to see me. *Really* see me.

This isn't an apology, like our impromptu lunch date, or a freak coincidence, like her bandaging my knife wound during the storm.

This is different. Something new.

"Yeah, you should really think it over. I'm not sure I'll be great company," she laughs self-deprecatingly.

I glance at the calendar tacked to the wall as I tap my fingers on the desk.

The music festival is tonight. Mia and I had planned to go to it together, but after our argument and this subsequent stalemate, I don't expect her to show up for the concert. She never wanted to go in the first place; she was only placating me.

Still, I can't invite Lare to be my "date."

"Um," I sigh, trying—vainly—to untangle my thoughts. I feel as if my head is full of knots. My hair actually *is* full of knots; I rake a hand back through it, grimacing and chewing on my bottom lip.

"There's this music festival going on tonight. It's called Vampire Rock Fest, imaginatively enough. A portion of the ticket proceeds goes toward funding vampire awareness, and my best friend is performing..." I'm babbling now, so I shake my head, cut to the chase. "It'll be fun," I say weakly, "and...I think you should check it out. Azure—that's my friend—her music is great."

"Oh...well, thank you for the recommendation, Courtney."

There are other voices talking in the

background on her end of the line again; I can make out something about *investigation* and *get to the bottom of this.*

Lare's tone is detached, formal, but regretful as she says, "I hope that I'll see you later."

"I hope so, too," I start—but the dial tone interrupts me.

Lare has already hung up.

That was...abrupt.

I sigh heavily, staring at the disconnected phone in my hand.

After a few moments, I wander out of the office and see David sweeping the floor—for the third time today. I'm about to tell him he can go home early—it's been a slow, customer-less afternoon—when I step alongside the counter and notice his backpack lying on the floor.

More specifically, I notice the *SANG* brochure sticking out of the front pocket of his backpack.

Immediately, my eyes flick up to David, watching him as he sweeps nonexistent dust bunnies and whistles that slick, too-catchy tune.

I'd like to believe someone shoved the brochure into his hands, that he didn't read it, that meant to throw it out.

That he's not allied with a hate group.

But I don't know what to believe about anyone anymore.

Chapter Seven: Vampire Kiss

I stare at my reflection in the mirror, tugging at various hems uncomfortably.

With my blonde hair and skin-tight black clothes, I feel like Sandy after her cool-girl transformation at the end of *Grease* — except that Sandy really *was* cool, and I'm just faking it, wearing my cool little sister's borrowed clothes.

I haven't worn a skirt this short since I was in elementary school. And I've *never* worn fishnet stockings in my life. The zippered tank top is sexy but so form-fitting that I feel as if I'm laced into a corset.

Seriously, are clothes supposed to *hurt*?

Doesn't matter. I'm running late, and I'm out of options. With a shallow sigh, I dig around in the back of my closet and drag out an old shoe box, a souvenir from my grunge phase. Smiling wistfully, I blow the dust off of the lid and open the box up. Inside, there they are — my black military-style boots, bought from an army surplus store for ten bucks when I was in eleventh grade.

I sit down on the edge of the bed and pull on the boots, lacing them up tightly over the fishnet stockings. When I stand up, the boot heels make satisfying *clomps* on my bedroom floorboards.

Back in front of the mirror, I pull at my hair, drawing it up into a high ponytail and tucking an errant curl behind my right ear. I apply some dark eye makeup, along with a little lip gloss and a spritz of my favorite perfume, a musky scent called Rendezvous.

The woman who stares back at me from the glass is unfamiliar, a stranger, though her gestures perfectly mirror my own. *Is that really me?* I shake my head at my reflection, heart beating too fast. I feel strange, like I'm playing dress-up. Surely everyone will see the bookworm hiding behind this goth-Cinderella makeover...

I glance at the alarm clock on my nightstand and swear. Azure's performing early in the set, and according to her text, she's scheduled to go onstage in about forty minutes. I'll be lucky to find a *parking* space in forty minutes, let alone run to the venue in time to catch her whole show.

"Be good, Colette," I tell my cat, patting her fluffy head as she stares up at me with wide, unblinking, judgmental eyes, as if to say, "You're really going out of the house in *that*? *Really*?"

I grab my purse and keys and lock the front door on my way out. The sunset in the west is throwing a gorgeous shade of purple onto the clouds overhead. Tearing my eyes from the sky, I fall into my car, jam the key into the ignition and turn it.

And nothing happens.

No sputter. No shudder.

Nothing.

"Oh, no. No, no, no, no... Come on, you hunk of junk, not *tonight*." I try the key again and—again—no luck.

My car is as silent as a toy Matchbox.

"Oh, no, no, no, *no*," I whisper, pressing my forehead to the steering wheel.

Think, *Courtney*.

Nearly everybody I know is at the concert. It's unlikely that any of them would hear my SOS phone call over the blare of live music.

As a last-ditch effort, I shove the key into the ignition again. This time, the engine sounds as if it's being crushed by a trash compactor, and the screech of metal-on-metal makes my ears ring. I bang my fists on the steering wheel with a growl of frustration.

Then: "We've got to stop meeting like this," comes a soft, velvety voice just beyond my open car window.

Lare.

And when I shift my gaze, when I see her silver eyes flashing, her full lips curving, and her sweet, enormous dog pushing his nose over the edge of the door, trying—and succeeding—to lick me with his long pink tongue, my tension melts away, replaced by something else, something much more pleasant: a liquid rush of warmth, peace, calm.

God, I'm happy to see her.

"Just another day in paradise." I sit back and offer her a wry smile. "How are you doing, Lare?"

"I'm very glad to run into you," she says, her voice a low purr of satisfaction as she plants her hands on her hips and flicks her mirrored gaze to my steering wheel. "This guy giving you trouble again?" She pats the side mirror and lifts a brow.

"A *lot* of trouble." I sigh, then toss my keys into my purse. "I was about to leave for the concert, but the engine refuses to start." Staring toward the offending hood, I bite my lip. "It kind of sounds like it's about to self-destruct."

"Well...one might suggest that our meeting here and now was fate, then." Lare tugs Van Helsing away from the door as I open it and step out. The fluffy beast bounds forward, shoving his nose under my hand, licking my wrist. I chuckle, ruffling the fur behind his floppy white ears.

I breathe out and glance up, meeting Lare's shining eyes. The sun has sunk below the horizon, so the sky has darkened to charcoal gray above our heads. We're standing between streetlamps, in shadows, but somehow her eyes still seem to glow. "Fate?" I ask in a small voice.

"Well, I was finishing up Helly's walk and

was about to get ready myself."

"You mean—"

"*Oui.* I planned on attending the concert, too. I could use the distraction." Her eyes, bright just a moment ago, now look haunted. Hunted.

I swallow. "Is everything all right?"

"Ah..." Lare blinks, shakes her head, tousling her coppery hair over her shoulders. She refocuses her stare, lingering over my lips. "It would be a pleasure to drive you to the concert, *ma belle*." As she gazes at me, her eyes soften again, and the worry lines creasing her forehead begin to fade away. "Would you like that, to go with me?"

"Yes. I...really would. Thank you, Lare," I say quietly, holding her rapt, steady gaze. I'm nervous, unsure of what to do with my hands, so I keep petting Helly's head and ears, and he leans hard against me, his tail thwacking the backs of my fishnets-clad legs.

"Well, good." Lare's smile is a sunrise; it makes me feel new and warm, down to my very last atom. "Then that's settled." She turns, tugging Helly behind her on his leash. "Come in with me while I get ready, Courtney. I won't take more than a moment, I promise."

I walk alongside Lare to the front door of her house, holding tightly to my purse strap, my boots clunking over the stones. With a barely suppressed shudder, I remember the sight of

Mia standing in my front yard, stabbing an angry finger toward this house, ordering me to avoid all contact with Lare.

Lare's car had been in the driveway then, but it was raining, pouring. Surely she hadn't seen, hadn't heard. I hope... It was a humiliating scene, yes, but—more importantly than that—it was motivated by a brand of blind hatred that shakes my flimsy faith in the human race. A hatred that could have deeply hurt Lare.

A hatred that destroyed, once and for all, my relationship with Mia.

Lare holds her front door open for me, and I duck my head as I cross over the threshold, feeling Lare's warm presence at my back. She unclips Van Helsing's leash and sets the great animal free; he turns around immediately and sits down in front of me in the narrow hallway, tongue lolling out of his mouth. I have no choice but to pay his toll, petting him to persuade him to let me pass. He gazes up at me with big, brown, adoring eyes.

"What a good boy."

At my words, he begins to pant, the perfect picture of canine contentment.

"Stop flirting with our guest, Helly," Lare laughs softly. To me, she says, "Come in, come in, please—and make yourself comfortable." She aims toward a room branching off from the main hallway, gesturing for me to follow. I inch around Van Helsing with a chuckle, tracing

Lare's footsteps. But when I pause in the doorway, my mouth goes dry.

This room...

It's Lare's bedroom.

I should have realized it was her bedroom, but my mind is operating at about ten-percent reliability. And if my brain were a computer, its screen would be frozen right now. Time to reboot.

I try to shove my hands into my pockets, but of course Sharon's miniskirt doesn't have pockets, so I cross my arms over my stomach and glance around the space self-consciously.

It's a spare but elegant room. Lovely, really. There's a tea-colored lace coverlet on the bed, and the walls are painted a soothing, pale shade of lavender. On top of the antique dresser sits a full-bloomed orchid in a painted Spanish pot. The orchid's flowers are such a soft, dreamy hue of purple that they take my breath away. A grow light is positioned just above the pot, and the light filtering through the petals makes them look as if they're glowing from within.

They're so beautiful...

But my eyes are drawn, as if by gravity, to a much more beautiful sight.

Lare stands beside her bed, and—with startling casualness—she peels off her lacy blue tank top, revealing the blush pink satin bra underneath.

I hold my breath, stunned; time stands

still. Motionless, I stare at her—I can't stop staring at her—and my heart knocks against my ribs as she turns away from me, unhooking the clasp on her tight black pants and pulling them down over her hips, shimmying her long legs free.

"Just give me a minute to get dressed," Lare says, smiling sweetly, and not at all shyly, at me over her bare shoulder. "You can sit down on the bed, if you'd like."

I lick my lips and consider sitting but find I can't quite convince my muscles to move. Every part of me is focused on her, on Lare: the soft slopes of her arms, the hourglass curves at her waist, the lean planes of her smooth, toned thighs... The way that her curls drift over her back, casting shadowy tendrils on her faintly pink skin.

The room is dim, the blinds drawn, the only illumination cast by the grow light on the dresser, but when Lare turns again, lips parted as if she's about to say something to me, a strange expression flickers over her face, and her eyes trail my length—slowly, languorously—taking in my appearance. And my uncomfortable, embarrassing, concert-going clothes.

"Wow," she breathes, her French accent thick, her eyes dark and wide. I hear her draw in a breath and then let it out in a quiet sigh. "Courtney..." She turns to face me fully, sharp teeth visible between her parted lips.

Beneath her gaze, I don't blush; I *burn*.

Lare, standing so strong, so sure, in only a bra and panties, rakes her gaze over me again, looking surprised, amazed, as if *I'm* the one who just undressed in front of her.

She's staring at me.

With...longing.

Just as I'm staring at her.

We watch one another, the warm air sizzling, *alive*, between us as I take in a deep breath, as I rock back on my heels, trying to lock my knees to prevent myself from collapsing to the floor. This is too much, too intense... Beneath the heat of her gaze, something hatches inside of me, something bursting to life—vital and thriving. It's *want*, want like I've never felt it before.

Lare licks her lips. "You look beautiful, Courtney," she tells me, her voice soft and low, her eyes glinting with silver shards.

I laugh self-consciously, shaking my head, even as my full-length blush deepens. "This is my sister's style, not mine." I glance down at myself and lift my shoulders in a dismissive shrug. "Sharon didn't want me to embarrass her at the concert, so she forced me to borrow her clothes." My lips twist to one side in a pained smile.

"The outfit suits you."

"I... Thank you. I appreciate the

compliment."

Lare's shimmering gaze lingers over me for a moment longer. My heart thunders wildly within me, its rhythm a stampede. I feel exposed, but more than that, I feel *seen*. As if those shifting silver-blue eyes can take in more than my surfaces, as if they can penetrate me to my deepest core.

After a slow, suspended moment, Lare turns away from me, almost regretfully.

"I...just need to change. One moment." Her words are a near whisper. With silent footsteps, she moves into her *en suite* bathroom and closes the door.

My knees feel so wobbly, so weak that all I want to do is sink down onto the edge of the bed, but that seems impossible now, inconceivable. I can't sit on Lare's bed, where she sleeps, dreams... I am already so bewitched. Under her heated gaze, I had begun to forget everything. I had begun to forget that Mia and I haven't officially broken up. I had begun to forget that I have principles. I have never cheated on anyone in my life, and I'm not going to start now, even if my girlfriend is cheating on me.

But when Lare steps out of the bathroom, my tenuous grasp on my principles begins to loosen again. I feel like a kid desperately trying to catch the kite string that slipped out of her fingers, and as more and more time passes, the kite grows smaller and smaller against the sky...

Lare is wearing a fitted black button-down shirt and skinny black jeans that taper at the ankles. Every hard line and muscle, every soft curve, is outlined, emphasized, by her outfit. Her red hair spills over her shoulders in shining waves, and her eyes are outlined in thin sweeps of black.

She looks sexy, confident, mysterious.

Like a rock star.

A vampire rock star.

"So..." Lare smiles at me disarmingly, lifting her chin as she steps forward, her eyes flashing with a sharp, dangerous glint of desire. My gaze fastens to her white, pointed teeth. "What do you think?" she asks me simply, spreading her arms wide before positioning her hands on her hips. "Will this do for the concert?"

"Yes," I tell her, mouth dry. "Yeah. I mean, you look...amazing."

"*Merci.*"

If circumstances were different... If there were no Mia between us, and if I were brave enough, daring enough, reckless enough, I would push Lare down on the bed right now. I would climb on top of her, claim her mouth, her neck, taste her, learn her—but I can't do that. I shouldn't even be *thinking* about doing that. I fist my hands at my sides and swallow; then I offer Lare a wavering smile. "My friend—my friend Azure," I force out, "she's going to go on stage soon, in about thirty minutes or so. We have to... I mean, if you don't mind, we should get on the road."

Lare lets out a small sigh, but she nods vaguely and straightens her back. "Yes, of course. Yes, we must go," she agrees quietly, sweeping a black clutch purse off of the bed and leading the way as we wend through the house and aim for the front door. She pats Helly's head and then slides her feet into a pair of knee-high, skin-tight boots before we go outside together.

Her car—two-door, violet, European—is sleek and expensive, in comical contrast to my mustard yellow clunker in the neighboring driveway. I gaze at Colonel Mustard forlornly. I suppose I should be grateful to that infuriating lemon, because if he hadn't refused to cooperate, I would have never experienced these sensual minutes with Lare. I wouldn't be sharing a car ride with her now.

I glance sidelong at my elegant companion, with her lustrous waves draping like satin against her cheek, with her lean silhouette clad all in black.

And something in me rises. Something forceful, determined, new.

Lare clicks the unlock button on her key ring, and I step forward, sweeping open her driver's-side door, feeling like a tuxedoed male lead in an old black-and-white movie. I'm tempted to say something cliché, like *milady* or *after you*, but I'm too nervous to speak; all of my energy is focused on maintaining some—admittedly small—semblance of coolness. So I hold my tongue as I hold the door, tilting my head with an impish smile and a raised brow, urging her with a nod of my head to climb inside of the car.

But Lare doesn't climb inside, and she doesn't return my smile. She meets my gaze with desire in her eyes—bare, hot, piercing desire.

For me.

She moves, leans forward, her hip now pressed against my hip, and for a still, sacred moment, I think/fear/hope/believe that she's going to close the distance between us and kiss me.

But, instead, she tears her eyes from mine and slides into the driver's seat, averting her gaze to the view through the windshield. "Thank you," says Lare, her voice low, husky.

Dazed, I close the door gently and walk around to the other side of the car, feeling hot and ashamed.

What the hell am I doing?

Flirting.

I'm *flirting*.

And I've got to stop.

It's time for some evasive action. "How is

everyone at work coping with the kidnappings?" I ask her, effectively killing the mood, once I've joined her in the car and fastened my seat belt.

Lare shakes her head as she turns on the engine; it purrs obediently, like any well-behaved engine should. "We've heard nothing, no news," she says, anguish softening her voice. "It has been so difficult, Courtney. Everyone goes about their daily tasks, but there is so much fear." Her face hardens as she pulls out onto the road. "Still, we must prevail. We must. The work we are doing is too important, and everyone knows this, which is why we continue on, day and night, as if nothing has happened. But we keep glancing over our shoulders, wondering," she says, wincing, voice raw, "who will be next."

"Lare, I'm so sorry." I reach across the space between us and place my hand on her denim-clad leg. A reassuring gesture, nothing more, performed out of mindless habit: I've done the same thing to Azure and Sharon countless times in the past, when they were in need of comfort.

But the moment my palm connects with Lare's thigh, a jolt of electricity lances my fingers, like a static shock gone nuclear, and I realize my mistake. A mistake that, for some reason, I can't correct. I feel as if there's a magnet locking my palm to her leg.

Lare pulls to a stop at the approaching red

light; then she licks her lips and, very deliberately, turns her head to look at me. That's all she does, *looks* at me, but a rush of desire burns through my veins. So sudden, so hot, I feel as if my blood is boiling...

The light turns green, and Lare's foot remains on the brake, and my hand remains on her thigh.

"The light's changed," I tell her softly.

"Oh." She blinks several times, as if she's coming out of a trance. Then she gazes up at the streetlight and presses down on the gas pedal, silent, propelling the car onward, toward our destination.

I feel the muscles of her leg moving beneath my palm, and it's too intimate, too *close*, so I draw my hand back and face forward, arms crossed tightly over my stomach.

The concert is at the Edge Dome, a sprawling music venue that used to be home to the local orchestra, before they were shut down due to low attendance. Now the arena, in an unfortunate twist of irony, is dedicated to local rock concerts and touring performances of big-name music stars. The Dome is situated at the very edge of the city, which gave it its name—and allows it to offer a lot of parking space to its ticket holders.

The parking attendant, wearing a fluorescent yellow vest, stands at the entrance of the huge lot, waving people in with an orange, hand-held flag. After driving past several packed aisles of bumper-to-bumper cars, Lare finds an empty space, swings into it, and we both hurriedly climb out, our boot heels clicking on the blacktop.

I draw a deep breath of night air into my lungs. The temperature cooled considerably during our drive, and that coolness brings me back to myself, clears my head, helps me focus.

You still have a girlfriend, I remind myself miserably, repeating the words in my head like a mantra as I glare toward the bright lights of the arena.

Apparently, the universe is compelled to remind me of my coupledom, as well.

Because Mia is waiting for me at the gate leading into the Dome.

I see her, and I feel the whole world fall away.

I'm floating like a soap bubble, weightless — and at any moment, I might pop.

No. This doesn't seem real. This can't be happening...

I don't want this. I don't want a confrontation. Not now. Not tonight.

But there's *going* to be a confrontation as soon as Mia catches a glimpse of the woman beside me. I could never forgive myself if Mia said something to wound Lare.

Lare, who's walking blithely at my side, unaware of my inner implosion. I glance at her, and she smiles softly, excitement sparkling in her silver-blue eyes. She looks so beautiful, so eager, and so deservedly relaxed.

No.

I won't *let Mia hurt Lare, not ever.*

"I can wait for you here, Lare." My voice sounds high, strained. "Why don't you go buy your ticket?" I gesture toward the ticket counter to our left.

But, already, it's too late.

I feel it—this sinking sensation in my stomach—before I see it: Mia, peering through the crowd with her wide, brown eyes, spotting us. *Both* of us.

"*What* are you doing?" Mia shouts, her rage audible even over the boom of the music vibrating from within the Dome.

"Oh, my God," I whisper, and Lare glances at me worriedly.

"What's wrong, Courtney?" she asks in her soft, smooth French accent.

I can't reply, can't shift my gaze. Mia stalks toward us stiffly, anger making her face pale to a corpse's pallor.

Reflexively, I step in front of Lare. I can feel my own anger rising, can taste its bile in my throat.

"Lare," I whisper through gritted teeth, "please go buy your ticket, okay?"

Lare's shimmering eyes narrow as she glances from me to Mia, who's making a beeline toward us, her fists balled, her brows narrowed darkly, as she *stomps, stomps, stomps* her high-heeled boots.

"Are you all right, Courtney?" Lare asks quietly.

"Yes. I mean, no, but..." I sigh, shaking my head, gaze still fixed on Mia's white, furious face. "Can you, um, give us a moment?" I shift my eyes to Lare, beseeching her, and she nods hesitantly, flicking her silver, flashing gaze to Mia once more before stepping away, angling toward the ticket counter with her hands shoved deep into her jeans pockets.

"Okay, Mia, you need to calm down," I whisper, when Mia stops in front of me, eyes wild and nostrils flaring.

She stares at me, chest rising and falling in a long, deep breath. When she speaks at last, her voice is sharp, curt. "I was supposed to come here with *you*, remember? We had a *date*." Lips curled up in a smirk, she makes a show of taking in my appearance, flicking her eyes over my length with a raised brow. "What is this, the new Courtney Banks? Here with your *new* girlfriend?"

"Mia, it isn't—"

"Are you sleeping with her?" she snaps, so loudly that Lare and the dozen people surrounding us could have easily heard her, though they are all too polite—or too distracted by the music—to glance our way.

"Look at you, all dressed up like a pretty goth princess." Mia crosses her arms as she rakes her eyes over me again, sneering. "Have you turned into a vampire groupie?"

"You're one to talk about *groupies*," I reply coldly. "You've become Drew Yarrow's sycophant."

As Mia takes a step back, hurt brightening her shadowed eyes, she lifts her chin and bares her neck, which I can't help but notice is covered in love bites. Hickies. Hickies that I certainly didn't give her.

They almost look like bruises.

My heart somersaults in my chest, but I gulp down my pain and whisper, "Quite a collection you've got there, Mia."

"What?" Following the direction of my gaze, Mia pales further and ducks her chin back down, awkwardly drawing up the hem of her t-shirt in a vain attempt to conceal her telltale throat. She shakes her head, eyes slitted furiously. "You know what, Courtney? You don't know anything about Drew and me!" She almost sounds petulant, like a little girl trying to convince her mother that sugar actually *is* good for her, that she *should* be allowed to eat an entire birthday cake if she that's what she wants to do.

I inhale a shaky breath, slammed by the realization—in one cold, hopeless moment—that everything that I had imagined Mia and Drew were doing with one another was probably eerily close to the truth.

"You're right," I say hoarsely, my eyes unfocused, my whole body chilled, covered in goosebumps. "I don't know anything about you, Mia. I thought I knew you." I search her face, trying to find some trace of the woman I once thought I loved. But there's nothing familiar about her. There's nothing for me to hold onto anymore.

"Well, people change," Mia mutters despondently, staring at her shoes.

"Yeah," I agree, in a stronger, more convicted tone, "they do. And I tried to talk to you about this before, Mia. I don't think there's any sense in second—or third—chances. We've used up all of our chances, both of us. It's time for us to admit to ourselves that we just don't work. We don't fit into one another's lives. There's just..." I lift my arms, letting them fall uselessly against my hips. "There's nothing left."

Mia's eyes are wide enough to rival the full moon rising above our heads. She takes a step nearer to me, begins to reach for my hand but stops herself, biting down on her lip. "I'm not sleeping with Drew, Courtney," she blurts out defensively. "If that's what this is about—"

"Don't—"

"Okay, yeah, we've *kissed*...and...and we've done a little more than kissing, but just a little. I swear. We haven't—"

"Just *stop*." My heart aches so sharply that I press my fingers to my chest. "We have to just...stop." I feel so hot; my head is pounding. The lights from the arena are blurs, zigzags of blue and red and green.

"Please, Courtney. I still love you—"

I choke out a hoarse laugh. "I don't even know what that means," I tell her, tears leaking from the corners of my eyes. "And I don't think you know, either."

We stand in uncomfortable silence for seconds that yawn into minutes. Finally, Mia's phone rings inside of her purse, *ding-dinging* loudly, startlingly. With a curse, she fishes her cell out of her bag and glances at the illuminated screen.

"Oh. I...I have to go. I'll...call you." Mia steps forward, tries to wrap her arms around me, tries to bring me close enough to kiss. Her face is tilted up toward mine, and her lips are parted, waiting...

I take a firm step backward, shaking my head. "No," I tell her quietly, my voice thick with sobs. "No. We're done, Mia. It's over."

"Over?" My ex-girlfriend's brown eyes flood with tears, and I'm suddenly seized by the urge to hug her, to comfort her, even though I'm the one causing her to feel this pain. But I can't hug her. I can't be soft, vulnerable.

I have to break the cycle, or we'll just keep

hurting each other, over and over again.

So I stand my ground, imagining myself a statue—immobile, unfeeling—though I'm acutely aware of the aching cavity in my chest, a black hole where my heart used to beat.

And then Mia is shaking her head, too, and she whirls around, away from me, running off in the direction of the parking lot.

I feel as if all of the air has been forced out of my lungs. I start to hyperventilate, bending over at the waist, drawing in deep swallows of cool air. From the corner of my eye, one last hot tear falls, streaking its way over my raw, reddened cheek.

And then Lare's there. *Lare*. I feel her beside me, soundless, wordless. I feel her like a warmth, like a guiding star. She curls her long fingers around my elbow, drawing me up and gazing at me with her impossible silver eyes. In the neon glow cast by the stage lights, her eyes look electric, full of glimmering sparks.

"I'm sorry," she murmurs, her voice as soft as her expression.

I nod resignedly. "You heard."

"I heard." She inhales through her nose, staring intensely into my eyes. "Should I go? Am I complicating things for you—"

"No, no," I say quickly, raking a tired hand through my hair. "This... None of this has anything to do with you." I breathe in and breathe out and try to smile. It's a weak attempt, but Lare's mouth curves slightly in response. And then I take another deep breath and slip my hand into hers, feeling her warm palm pressed against mine. It's...comforting. It feels right.

"Come on," I sigh. "Let's go bang our heads or crowd-surf or...stand in the back with the other old people and tap our feet, listening politely."

Lare's smile widens, and as we face one another, she lifts her hand; slowly, softly, she wipes the stray tear from my cheek. "You have eyes like forests, Courtney," Lare whispers, her voice husky, her eyes brimming with something unspoken. "I think you can be wild, when you want to be. *Oui?*"

My heart—which, only a moment ago, had felt insubstantial, nonexistent—beats triple time in reply to Lare's words. I swallow and then laugh self-deprecatingly. "Oh, no, I'm not wild. Unless, by *wild,* you mean staying up past eleven on a work night to finish reading *Jane Eyre.*"

Lare raises a brow, lowers her voice, and then, as if in a dream, she whispers to me, "You, Jane, I must have you for my own—entirely my own."

I stare at her, lips parted, heart thundering, chest constricted as desire blazes, reborn phoenix-like inside of me.

Lare just quoted my favorite line from my favorite book. A line she knew by heart.

She smiles disarmingly, tilting her coppery head to one side. "Believe it not," she says, her brow still raised, "I played Mr. Rochester in a stage production of *Jane Eyre* at my women's college...once upon a time. I was quite fond of the cravat."

"...oh."

I'm so surprised, so flustered that I go into Robo Courtney mode, automatically following Lare as we move toward the line and then hand our tickets over to the bouncer at the gate. We make our way through the crowd inside of the Dome itself, trying to find—i.e. shove our way into—a place in the audience.

"Do you enjoy acting?" I shout to Lare over the music; the floor beneath our feet is shaking.

She laughs, bringing her lips close to my ear. "No, but some friends of mine dared me to audition for the part. And I never turn down a dare."

Despite the strobing lights and the ear-splitting music, I pause in the flow of hot, pushing bodies, feeling a time-out-of-time moment as I meet Lare's gaze. She's returning my stare meaningfully, and then she inclines her face toward mine, brushing her mouth against my ear. "I never turn down a dare," she repeats, and I can hear the smile, the *dare*, in her voice. "For future reference."

Suddenly, the music that has been

booming all around us *stops*—for a long, drawn-out moment. Someone shouts indecipherable words into a microphone, and then, just as unexpectedly, the music starts up again, but there's a different vibe to the melody, something fresher, wilder. The crowd erupts into frantic, delighted screaming.

In all honesty, I'm only peripherally aware of the shifting waves of sound, but I'm all too aware of Lare's nearness, her scent, her thigh hot against mine. We're still holding hands, and every so often, Lare caresses the back of my hand with her thumb, invoking lightning bolts of longing within me.

We've positioned ourselves several feet away from the stage, but I recognize Azure the instant she struts out in front of the crowd—purple-mohawked and drop-dead gorgeous in a black-sequined jumpsuit—and that's when I shake my head, command myself to be here, now, to *pay attention*.

"That's her, isn't it?" Lare asks excitedly. "Azure?"

I nod my head. "Yeah, the acts must be running late. We got here just in time."

Lare lifts a brow, whispers, "Fate," into my ear—and I inhale deeply, staring at my reflection in her mirrored eyes.

Azure grabs the microphone with rock-star confidence, and when she belts out the first verse of her first song—a classic called *The*

Straight White Male's Lament; JK, LOL — the concertgoers cheer, jumping up and down and waving their hands above their heads. Caught up in the adrenaline rush, I scream my heart out for Azure as she dances, moonwalks — she tried to teach me how to moonwalk once...*once* — and sings until she nearly goes hoarse.

She's incredible on stage. Charismatic, sexy, funny... As her best friend, I'm biased, granted — but I'm hardly her only fan. There are women throwing phone numbers and bras onto the stage, and a bouncer has to physically restrain a young lady from climbing over the speakers to fling herself at Azure, though she keeps screaming, "I love you!" even as she's dragged away upside-down.

Lare appreciates the music, too. She's bouncing on the balls of her feet, whistling through her fingers. She looks odd, different, and it takes me a moment to realize that she looks different to me because — in this moment, at least — she isn't worried about anything.

She's simply happy.

And she looks radiant when she's happy, like a luminous, red-haired angel in a Botticelli painting, no cares in the world.

I make a vow, then and there, to try my best to inspire this state of happiness for her whenever I have the opportunity. The tension that she's been experiencing for the past couple of weeks has taken too high of a toll.

After the concert, and after we drive to my house, with the explosively loud music still ringing in my ears, Lare eases her car into my driveway, her bumper braking just behind Colonel Mustard. She leans back in her seat, tilting her head toward me with a warm smile.

"Thank you for tonight, Courtney," she says softly, drawing me in with those shining eyes. "I really needed something like that." Her voice is hoarse.

I shake my head with a small smile. "Don't thank me. I needed it, too." I lick my lips as I hold Lare's gaze. One of her arms is pillowed beneath her head, and her stare smolders as she regards me, indulgently, lazily, her eyes raking over my length with slow, bare appreciation.

Maybe I'm still hyped up on the energy of the concert. Maybe the now-confirmed fact that Mia cheated on me has finally sunk in, settled like a old rubber boot on the bottom of the sea, and ceased kicking me in the gut with every breath I take. Maybe the way that Lare is studying me, the way that the silver in her eyes catches the moonlight, is making me feel wild, fairy-charmed, enchanted.

I surprise myself by leaning across the space between us. Again, I place my hand on Lare's thigh, but this time—we both know—my gesture isn't one of comfort. I trace my fingertips lightly over the fabric of her pants, holding her gaze as her mouth opens, as she softly inhales. Her heat radiates into my palm, igniting something inside of me.

Everything within me aches for Lare. She makes me feel wonder and excitement and raw, real desire.

I can't deny this anymore.

So, impulsively, breathlessly, I brush my mouth against hers.

As far as kisses go, it's light, barely there. A question of a kiss. "Do you want this, too?" my lips ask, their contact feather-light.

I want her to want it.

And — thank God — she does.

Lare wraps her arms around my shoulders, and the gear shift presses against my hip as our mouths crash together. I feel her sharp teeth on my lips, my tongue. Suddenly, I'm all heat, all longing. Lare's fingers curl into my hair, her arms tighten around me, and we dedicate ourselves to this kiss — one kiss, single, hungry, endless.

My hand cups her cheek, and then I trace her jaw, gliding my fingertips along the side of her warm neck, her skin so soft, so hot.

When we part hours, minutes, or seconds later, I'm panting. Lare's eyes are dark with desire as she gazes at me. She studies me for a moment, one brow raised, and then she flicks her flashing eyes toward her house.

"Would you like to go inside and — " she

begins, but her last word is clipped; she falls silent. She's staring at something, and—eyes wide—she closes her mouth, straightens her shoulders.

I follow her gaze.

No.

No, no, no.

And just like that, the memory of our kiss begins to fade, replaced by a sight that I can hardly make sense of. I blink at it as I sit in my seat—in shock, speechless, wringing my hands, shaking my head.

Vandalism. On the front of Lare's house, the words *I know what you did* are spray-painted in bright, jagged blue paint. Whoever did this stood, brazen, on Lare's lawn and scrawled the words in plain sight, where anyone might have seen—any neighbor, any passerby. *Anyone* could have seen, and someone probably *did* see, and no one stopped it from happening. No one stood up for Lare.

"Oh, my God," I whisper, as Lare and I reach for our door handles at the same time and climb out of the car, walking over to her driveway to stare at the ugly graffiti with our mouths hanging open. We're silent, dumbstruck.

I know what you did? What the hell could that mean?

Lare takes a deep breath and fists her hands on her hips, jaw set, her eyes solid mirrors beneath the glow of the streetlamps.

"Lare." I thread my fingers through hers, squeezing her hand gently.

She gazes at me with a distant, hollow gaze. "It's... It's all right. Don't trouble yourself, Courtney. This isn't a big deal. Only...a small one." Her voice is gruff. She sighs and rakes a hand through her long, red hair. Suddenly, she looks weary, lifeless, not at all like the vibrant, passionate woman who was kissing me in the car a moment ago. "I must call the police," she says, pulling her phone from the back pocket of her pants. "No," she pauses, narrowing her brows. "First I have to make certain that Helly is okay, that they didn't break into the house—"

"I'll call the police, Lare. Don't worry about that. You go check on Van Helsing."

She offers me a grateful half-smile, the most she can muster, I assume, at this point in time. "Thank you."

I begin to dial the police station as Lare unlocks her front door, and I follow her inside with the phone pressed to my ear. She tries to wave me back, but I shake my head, doggedly persisting her. Because what if the vandal is still here? There's a slim chance that he or she would be stupid enough to stick around, but just in case, I don't want Lare to confront an intruder alone.

My stomach twists as I listen to the phone ring. I think about the kidnappings from Give

Life Technologies. I think about the people who hate vampires, who want them demeaned, punished, dead. I think about the fact that Lare isn't safe, and that I don't know how to protect her.

"Hello?" I say, when a bored-sounding policeman picks up my call.

"How can I help you, ma'am?" he drawls into the receiver, making wet, slurping sounds. He must be drinking something. Coffee, most likely, given the late hour. "What's going on?" His voice is young, sleepy.

"My..." I stop, tongue-tied, uncertain as to what I should call Lare. "My friend Lare's house has just been vandalized," I say into the receiver, wincing. I take a deep breath, soldier on: "She's a vampire, and someone spray-painted the front of her house."

"Vampire, eh?" the guy snorts.

I grit my teeth, squeeze the phone, realizing, too late, that I shouldn't have mentioned the word *vampire* at all.

"Look, her house has been *vandalized*. Could you send someone to – "

"Lady, we're real busy here tonight." He makes a show of yawning loudly, and I can almost *hear* him rolling his eyes. "We can get a squad car over there in the morning."

"The morning?" I blink, then glare at the phone for a moment, trying to suppress my anger. I'm standing in the lamplight of the

211

living room; Lare has moved into the kitchen, where I can hear her speaking softly to her dog. "But what if she's in danger? What if—" I swallow, wide-eyed, disbelieving. "Would you send a car out tonight if it were a human's house that had been vandalized?"

"Eh... Dunno. Maybe yes, maybe no. Like I said, it's a busy night." His tone is simpering; I think he's actually *smiling*. "Just gimme the details, and we'll be out first thing in the A.M., okey-dokey?"

I answer his questions through clenched teeth and manage to keep my temper in check, but when I hang up the phone, the injustice, the absence of decency, of kindness, of empathy spikes my blood pressure sky high. My body is coursing with adrenaline—from the vandalism, from the kiss. I grip my temples.

This is all too much.

"Look," I tell Lare, who's kneeling on the floor in her kitchen and gently massaging the area behind Van Helsing's ears. He's sitting before her with a dopey dog smile, thumping his tail against the tiled floor. "It isn't safe for you to stay here tonight."

She regards me with haunted silver-blue eyes.

I exhale heavily, dropping my phone back into my purse. Then I crouch down next to her and rest a hand on her shoulder. "Lare, something terrible could happen if you stay here. What if the vandal comes back? The police refuse to do anything until morning." I press my lips together, hard, breathing out through my nose.

"Because I'm a vampire, right?" Her mouth curves softly, bitterly. "That's why they won't come right now?"

I bow my head.

"I heard you on the phone," she says, with a small, sad smile. "I'm sorry. I should have warned you not to say anything about—" She shakes her head, staring down at Helly with a forlorn expression. Her hair drifts from her shoulder, obscuring her face. "The police in this city aren't disposed to serve and protect people like me."

My heart constricts in my chest, and I can feel tears gathering at the corners of my eyes. "But that's so unfair—"

"It's all right, Courtney," she tells me soothingly, wrapping her arms around me in a warm embrace. I hug her back, holding her tight against me.

"It's *not* all right. God, I'm so sorry. I wish there was something I could *do*." My cheek against her shoulder, I take a deep breath, inhaling Lare's sweet perfume.

"Being here with me now is enough, more than enough," she whispers, pressing her lips to my forehead. We remain in that position for a long moment, tiredly supporting one another, reluctant to let go. The rhythm of her heartbeat calms me, and I find myself breathing easier, relaxing slightly. My head begins to clear.

"Please," I say then, hoarsely, sitting up and searching her face. "Stay with me tonight. Not for...not for any other reason than that I want to make certain you're safe," I finish weakly. I swallow the lump in my throat and await her answer.

After a moment's consideration, Lare nods. She looks drained, exhausted. "That's kind of you. Thank you, Courtney."

"Good. It's settled. Come on, Helly," I tell the big dog, gathering his leash from the floor, where it lay coiled. We walk quietly together through the living room, and then, after Lare locks her front door, the vampire, Saint Bernard and I make the short trek to my house.

I rummage around in my drawers until I find my most comfortable pair of pajamas—the ones covered in sepia illustrations of books—and lend them to Lare, who considers them with a quiet, tired grace, a soft smile, and simply says, "*Merci.*"

"Sure. Um, you can head upstairs to the bathroom to change, freshen up..."

"Okay." Lare nods and aims for the steps.

To feel useful, I look after Van Helsing, setting him up in his own room—my guest bedroom. I fill a mixing bowl with water and carry it up the stairs, placing it beside him. He laps at it for a moment; then he wags his tail, gazing up at me in adoration. I tug the comforter off of the bed and spread it out on the floor. He snuffles it appreciatively, pawing at its folds until he's satisfied by the messy configuration. Then he flops down with a sigh.

The door is open, and Colette, who has never met a dog in her life, fluffs up to ten times her normal size at sight of our new, very large animal guest. Her tail is puffed out like a bottle brush, and the fur on her back is standing up in a straight line. And yet, despite the fact that she obviously loathes Van Helsing's presence, Colette dashes into the room and darts under the guest bed.

Cat logic.

"*Why?*" I moan, crouching down to peer under the mattress. "Colette, you crazy cat, you just ran into the same room as the animal you're terrified of," I remind her in soft, soothing tones. I've always believed that Colette understands human speech, but, if she does possess that superpower, she isn't putting it to use now. Instead, she's yowling and staring at Van Helsing's paws as if they're locked-and-loaded weapons of mass destruction.

I sigh again, rising up to a kneel and half-collapsing onto the bed. I'm too tired to deal with this. But if I don't get my panicked Colette out of this room, she's probably going to need therapy. And poor Helly will *definitely* need therapy.

"Is my boy giving you trouble?" asks Lare from the doorway.

"No, he's—" I glance over my shoulder, and then I sink down onto my heels—because my legs are far too weak to hold me up any longer. I swallow as my heart beats like a hammer in my chest.

I suppose it's very French to undress in front of other people without shyness, as Lare demonstrated before the concert. It is probably, therefore, *also* very French to be nonchalant about buttoning your button-up pajama top.

Because Lare hasn't buttoned the pajama shirt yet, revealing an inch-wide strip of rosy-tinged skin that looks warm and satin-soft...

I lick my lips, blink a few times, and try to focus on the task at hand as Lare begins to button the shirt slowly, her fingers moving from the bottom up. She must have been in the middle of changing, heard Colette's banshee wails, and came out of the bathroom to see what she could do to help.

Lare crosses the room and sinks down beside me on the floor, holding my gaze and leaning forward. I can't help but notice that she left the top three buttons undone: the pink swell of her breasts draws my eyes like a gravity.

"Let's try to lure her out together, shall we?" says Lare. Her lips curl up at the corners knowingly—as if she realizes where my eyes have trespassed.

I draw in a deep breath and place my hand over hers. "You're amazing."

She tilts her head, smile widening. "How so?"

"If my house had been vandalized, I would... I would be like Colette here, yowling under the bed. But you're calm, collected, brave..." I trail off, gazing at her in wonder.

Lare says nothing for a long moment, only studies me, her eyes flickering with something I can't read, her lips parted, her breath coming in a soft, steady rhythm that makes my heart forget how to beat.

"I am not brave, *ma chere*," she says quietly, at last. "I only do what must be done. It's a skill I've learned, had to learn, over the years. But, tonight, I'm in this house. Your house. With you. And that makes up for a great deal of heartache."

I hold her gaze, unblinking, breathless.

And this time, it's Lare who leans forward, who presses her mouth against mine, her lips hot and sweet. This kiss is softer than the one in the car—quieter, almost. Maybe because it's Lare who's taking the lead, Lare who's moving her tongue against mine, who's kissing me with warmth and grace as I wrap my arms around her neck and press my body against hers.

Still kissing, we rise instinctually, moving

onto the guest bed, lying down on our sides in gradual motions, face to face. Lare smiles against me, and her pointed incisors graze my bottom lip; I shudder against her. The teeth are sharp, but they trail over my skin like sheathed knives, incapable of harm, unwilling to commit harm. I know they could hurt me. They exist to bite.

But I trust Lare wholly.

Colette growls again under the bed, and it's only then that we draw apart, laughing together, sitting up. I chuckle, embarrassed, as Colette dashes out between my feet, disappearing through the open bedroom door and making a beeline for my room—and, I imagine, the sanctuary that awaits her under my bed.

I sigh, rake a hand through my messy hair. "Look," I tell Lare then, reaching out to tuck an errant red strand behind her ear. My fingers linger against her face, and she tilts her head to rest her cheek against my hand. "It's been a long day. For both of us," I whisper, smiling softly at her. "Why don't we just go to bed? We'll talk in the morning, figure out what to do then about the house and...and everything else."

"I would like that, Courtney," Lare says, her voice a velvety purr of exhaustion. She smiles fondly at me. Then she takes up my hand and draws it up to her mouth, pressing a soft kiss against the center of my palm. "I would like that very much," she murmurs, the growl in her voice making my skin shiver with goosebumps.

Electricity zaps through my sleepy limbs, desire moving through me like a supercharged current...

But I don't want our first time to be like this: exhausted, falling together to hush the unfairness of the world lurking outside of our embrace. I don't want to associate our first time with vandalism, with fear, with hate.

So I do one of the hardest things I've ever done. I force myself to rise, to let her go. "Until tomorrow," I tell her regretfully.

Lare says nothing, but she watches me with her flickering gaze until I close the guest bedroom door behind me.

The Vampire Next Door

Chapter Eight: You Think You Know Someone

When I wake up, I'm sore all over, and my ears feel as if they're stuffed with cotton, or like there's a white noise machine playing inside of my head. After a groggy moment, I realize that I slept in, that the sunshine filtering over the bedspread is a warm, golden, late morning glow.

I blink and peer at the clock: it's fifteen past ten. I massage the back of my neck and stare up at the ceiling. Well, I must have needed the sleep. After all, it was a hell of a night.

I remember Mia, angry at first, and then sobbing, running away from me after we broke up. I remember the concert, the ear-blasting music, the throbbing bass, and Azure strutting across the stage as if the world belonged to her—because, for an hour, it kind of did. A rush of love and pride fills my chest. She was incredible, magnetic. My best friend, the rock star.

I remember the vandalism, my fury toward the police officer and the bigoted world at large. Those words haunt me—*I know what you did*—sketched out in brilliant blue. I dreamed of that phrase last night, appearing everywhere I looked: on the walls, the windows, and the mirror, streaked across my reflection.

I shake my head, pushing the dream back into my subconscious.

Because the moments that I remember more clearly than anything else from last night are the kisses that I shared with Lare.

I reach up, press my fingertips to my lips. They're sore, too, but it's a delicious soreness, one that I hope lingers, reminding me of the taste of her mouth...

God, I feel a little loopy—and a lot hot and bothered.

Right. A cold shower is in order if I'm going to make it through the rest of the day.

Flustered, I roll out of bed, wondering if Lare is still lying in my guest room, her coppery hair fanned over the pillow...or if, more likely, she woke up hours ago. Maybe she's not even in my house anymore; the policeman did tell me that he'd send a car over in the morning to check out the scene of the crime.

I shuffle out of the bedroom—nearly tripping over Colette—and stumble across the hallway toward the bathroom. I tap the halfway-open door absentmindedly and—

Lare's standing there, wringing her hair out in a towel.

She's very nude. And very wet.

"Oh," I say, in a short outtake of breath.

Lare glances toward me, and a slow, sensual smile slinks over her face. She's not blushing at all. Granted, I'm doing more than enough blushing for the both of us.

"*Bonjour.*" She straightens a little, shaking her wet hair over her shoulders. "My house has been cordoned off by the police. I should have asked first, but I hope that you don't mind that I took a shower?"

"Oh, no. No, that's...fine. *Mi casa es su casa,*" I stammer—because apparently, when I'm nervous, I slip into high-school Spanish. Face on fire, I try to avoid staring at her goddess-like breasts, her hourglass hips...

Lare lifts her chin, her smile widening as she drops the towel in her hands to the floor.

Frantically, I try to think of something to say. "Have you had breakfast yet—er, I mean, your, um, drink?"

"Yes, I drank this morning. I went to my house for some clothes and spoke with the police when they arrived," she says, shrugging elegantly, comfortably.

"And what did the police say?" I ask her, suddenly anxious. I wish I had woken up sooner, so that I could have stood by her side when she confronted the police.

"They said what I expected: that they didn't have any leads, but they'd let me know if they discovered clues related to the case. Which I doubt they will." She crosses her arms at her waist.

"It's all so frustrating."

"Yes. It is."

For a long moment, we don't say anything more, only face one another—Lare with one brow raised, a smile teasing at her lips, while I war with the urge to step forward and gather her in my arms...

I hear a light *ding* from the kitchen. My phone.

"Sorry. Just a minute," I say, leaving her and hurrying downstairs with an odd mixture of relief and regret.

My cell, which I must have dropped on the kitchen counter when we came in last night, dings insistently until I take it up, staring down at the number on the screen.

"Hi, Sharon," I greet my sister, pressing the phone to my ear. "What's—"

"Courtney? Courtney, something terrible happened." Sharon sounds distressed, her voice high-pitched and breathy, as if she's been running—or crying. "There was an attempted kidnapping at the vampire club."

Another kidnapping?

"Are you okay?" I ask her, gripping the phone.

"I'm all right. I'm all right, seriously," she repeats quickly. "We went to the club after the concert last night, and someone tried to take Marta when she went into the lady's room. I saw it happen, but the guy got out through the back door."

"Marta?" I blink. Marta is a mutual friend, a poet. And a human. Everyone who was kidnapped from Give Life Technologies was human, too. Could there be a connection? Have the police made the connection?

I swallow as a shiver runs down my spine.

"Courtney, Marcus and I were taken to the police station for questioning. We've been here all night. Could you come and—"

"God, I'll be there in an instant. Like, *half* an instant. Don't worry. I'm so glad you're safe," I tell her, all in one breath. "I'll be right there, okay?"

"Thanks, sis. See you soon."

I end the call and turn on my heel to seek out Lare, but she's already behind me, leaning back against the counter, clothed in a silky lavender blouse and skinny black pants. Her hair is still damp and drawn back from her shoulders. She indicates the phone with a nod of her head.

"Trouble?" she murmurs.

"Yeah. An attempted kidnapping of a human from a vampire club last night." I watch her reaction, biting my lip as her silver-blue eyes widen. "My sister and her boyfriend Marcus were there, and they were taken to the police station for questioning. Marcus—he's a vampire."

Lare's gaze flashes with understanding.

I sigh. "I have to go pick them up."

"I can drive you to the police station—"

"No, Lare." I take a step nearer to her and touch her cheek with my hand. We're so close now that my breasts are grazing against hers—but lightly. Too lightly. I sigh, inhaling the sweet, intoxicating scent of the beautiful woman before me. "I don't want you mixed up in any of this," I whisper, gliding my hand to her chin. "Not after what happened last night."

She holds my gaze, frowning as if she's going to be stubborn, going to insist on accompanying me, despite my argument—but then she's pressing her car keys into my free hand and closing my fingers over the warm metal.

"If you won't let me come with you, you must take my car." She holds up a finger. "No protests, hmm? After all, you don't know if your car will start."

I draw in a deep breath. "Thank you."

Lare leans forward to brush her lips against my forehead. "Come back soon, *ma chere*."

Ma chere. A pleasant, floaty sensation fills my chest—before reality slams back into me, as heavy as an avalanche of bricks. And, I don't know, pianos. "What will you do while I'm gone? Will you stay here?" I ask her encouragingly, staring into her shining eyes. "The police have been no help. We don't know if your house is safe yet."

Lare nods thoughtfully, leans back against the counter. "I suppose I'll find out if Van Helsing and Colette can become friends..." She grins.

I laugh doubtfully. "Good luck."

And then I dash upstairs, leap out of my pajamas, and throw on some jeans and a t-shirt. My hair is a tangled blonde cloud surrounding my head; I look like a time traveler from the 1980s. There's no hope of making my messy mane presentable, so I pull it all back into a sloppy bun. Within the space of a minute, I'm grabbing my phone and my purse, and then I'm out the door, buckling myself into Lare's purple car.

The drive to the station feels as if it takes eons, ages—but maybe that's only because I'm so impatient to arrive. When I finally park in front of the large brick building and hurl myself out of the car, I'm so frazzled that I nearly forget to take the keys out of the ignition. Then I pause, catching my breath, leaning against the door to absorb the scene before me: there's a crowd of people loitering in front of the station. On a Saturday? I wrinkle my brow, squinting. It's then that I notice several people are holding up signs, milling around the entrance as if they're protesting something.

"Oh, no..." My stomach plunges down to the earth's core. "SANG," I curse under my breath, jogging toward the police station anxiously.

Some of the protesters are wearing jackets that have SANG emblazoned across the backs in neat embroidery — next to a cartoonish image of a gigantic vampire stake. I refuse to acknowledge the hate-filled signs as I trot up the steps, but once I'm inside and running through the hallway, I confront a shouting match — centered around my little sister.

Surrounded by a tight knot of people, Sharon is wailing, raging, reaching out with clawing hands. I blink, stunned by the feral anger in her green, black-outlined eyes. Her waist is encircled by her boyfriend's arm, and Marcus himself looks pale, withdrawn, as he clings to Sharon, restraining her from launching herself at the person standing in front of her.

With eyes as wide as saucers, I run closer. My mouth is dry, and my palms are sweating. I feel an adrenaline burst to help Marcus and Sharon, but there's also a cold, slithering dread in my gut. Beyond Sharon's participation in it, there's something deeply unsettling about the sight before me. I feel it before I understand the root cause of it: Sharon is screaming at the top of her lungs, yelling expletives at a blonde woman I only recognize from the news — though I've had nightmares about her often enough.

Drew Yarrow, the leader of SANG, the brainwasher/seducer of my ex-girlfriend, stands mere feet away from me—finally, in the flesh.

She's slightly shorter than me, but what she lacks in height, she makes up for in presence. She has luminescent, pale blonde hair, board straight and cut severely at her chin. She's wearing a tight gray pencil skirt and a tight white blouse that frames her ample cleavage. Drew looks professional, like the lawyer that she is, but her eyes—despite their masterful makeup—are sinister, dangerous, narrowed to slits as she glares at my sister.

At last, she parts her red lips and says, "Being surrounded by *animals* has brought out the beast in you, young lady." Her words, spoken in a low, level voice, are directed toward Sharon, and they set my sister off on another impressive swearing tirade.

Drew is flanked by several slack-jawed members of SANG; they remind me of drone bees clustered around a queen. There is something regal about Drew, admittedly—but she would be the sort of queen who would guillotine you for stealing a loaf of bread, or for serving her bread on the wrong fancy plate.

Now Drew lifts her chin, sneering at both Marcus and Sharon. "Bedding one of those creatures makes you just as despicable as they are." With that, she turns to share a laugh with the person closest to her, a person who, until now, had been blocked from my sight by Drew's body.

Mia.

Mia, staring at Drew adoringly. No, *adoringly* isn't the right word; it isn't strong enough, not by half. Mia looks rapturous, hypnotized, like an ecstatic congregation member at an evangelism rally.

My ex-girlfriend's rapt, wide brown eyes don't slip from Drew's commanding aura for a moment, so she doesn't see me, doesn't know I'm here.

I draw in a deep breath to calm my galloping heart. It's irrelevant, Mia's presence. Even Drew's presence doesn't matter. I can't change either of their minds; I can't show them the evil of their hate-mongering ways. Besides, that's not why I'm here.

I'm here to help my sister.

"Sharon, stop, " I force out, squeezing between shoulders and elbows until I'm standing beside my sister and Marcus. The instant that Sharon sees me, she goes silent, but her face takes on a pinched look as she shifts her gaze past me, still glaring at Drew. If Sharon's eyeballs could shoot laser beams, Drew would be on the floor right now, toppled over like a bowling pin.

I turn my attention to Mia, and Mia looks at me, too, but her gaze is empty, unseeing, like the dead eyes of a porcelain doll. It makes my stomach turn, witnessing how much Drew has changed her, manipulated her.

Drew herself *does* see me. And somehow she recognizes me, though we've never met before in our lives, because she smiles cruelly, tipping Mia's chin upward with one long, manicured nail. Drew Yarrow bends down and kisses Mia deeply, then, passionately, while the ruckus around her gradually ebbs.

Mia says nothing when their mouths part, only squeezes Drew's arm and recommences staring at the sharp-faced woman as if she's a saint—or a goddess made flesh.

"You *asshole!*" Sharon shouts at Mia over my shoulder. "You *slime!* How could you do this to my sister? What's *wrong* with you? I *knew* she was too good for you!"

"Sharon—"

"Courtney, did you see what she just—"

"Forget about her. Please. It doesn't matter, not anymore," I say quickly, quietly. "Now tell me—what's going on?" I position myself to block her view of Drew and Mia and place my hands on her shoulders, holding her in place.

Sharon huffs. "Mia is such a—"

I shake my head only once, and my sister bites her tongue and narrows her eyes, growling in frustration. "What's happening?" I ask her again.

"Okay, fine. Drew *Yarrow*," she begins,

rising on her tiptoes to peer at the woman over my shoulder, "was seen talking to Marta at the club last night, and since Marta is still out of it because of the stuff that was slipped into her drink, Drew was brought into the station for questioning."

I cast a glance to Drew. She's facing away from us now, speaking in a low voice with the press, who are holding their microphones or voice recorders out to her while she smiles widely, graciously, into the lone video camera.

"That vampire and his shrewish cohort, as you just saw, were verbally and physically attacking me," Drew announces to the camera crew, oozing an oily, lawyerly charm. "They're as undomesticated as wild animals. Clearly a threat to the safety of this city."

"*What* did you say?" Sharon starts with a snarl, but Marcus and I close our hands over her arms, simultaneously shaking our heads.

"Come on, Sharon," I mutter. "We have to get out of here. Away from *them*."

Sharon gives me a sour look, but then she sighs and nods. "Okay. Yeah, we're done. The police have our statements. The questioning took forever, because Marcus is a vampire." She rolls her eyes. "A fact which the cops brought up exactly eleven billion times..."

The three of us stalk past Drew, who smiles broadly as she talks on to the news reporters about the "vampire agenda." I stifle my fury, though I feel like an atomic bomb three seconds away from exploding. How could *anyone* take that woman seriously? Can't they see the eerie, unnatural glint in her eyes?

We *really* need to go outside, as far away from the police station—and, more specifically, Drew Yarrow—as possible.

But before we reach the door, I suffer a moment of weakness: I glance back for one last look at Mia. Her arms are locked around Drew's neck, tightly, desperately, as if Drew is her flotation device in an angry, stormy sea.

Suddenly, I'm compelled to turn around fully, to stop in my tracks, though I'm not sure why. I just can't stop staring at Mia's arms, Mia's hands. Mia's fingers...stained bright blue.

"Hey, I thought we were leaving," Sharon calls out to me. She's holding open the door with one hand, and Marcus is already waiting on the steps outside, ducking his head so that the SANG protesters won't catch sight of his telltale eyes or teeth.

"Coming," I say automatically. My mind reels as I follow my sister and her boyfriend into the sun. I feel numb, stunned, mute. I unlock Lare's car, and after we pile onto the seats, after I turn on the engine, the stuck gears in my brain come loose, creak, begin to turn again. What I saw and what I know finally click into place.

Mia's fingers were *blue*.

The words spray-painted on Lare's house

were *blue.*

Is it possible? Could *Mia* have vandalized Lare's house? *Would* she have done something like that, something so stupid, so reckless, so motivated by blind hatred? And, if she did spray-paint those words, what the hell could they possibly mean?

"Hey, when'd you get a new car?" Sharon asks, yanking me back to the present moment.

"Um..." I cough into my hand; my voice is hoarse with emotion. "It's not mine. It's Lare's," I tell her, casting her a glance. Sharon stares at me blankly, so I clear my throat and say, "Remember? The woman I was telling you about?"

She's still staring, uncertain. Well, Sharon did have a long night, didn't get any sleep, so I smile slightly and shake my head, try again, "The vampire next door?"

"*O-o-o-o-oh.*" An expression of satisfaction breaks out over Sharon's face, and then she exchanges a look with Marcus, who's sitting behind her in the backseat. Sharon flops tiredly against the plush headrest and tosses a smile at me. "That's great, Court. I'm happy for you."

"Thanks, but..." I trail off, too tired to explain that Lare and I aren't exactly a *couple*. Not yet. I don't even have the energy to come to terms with the fact that the woman I was in a relationship with for four months has become someone else entirely, someone unrecognizable. Cheating is bad enough, but if Mia vandalized Lare's house, she's a perfect stranger to me, a person I never knew, and never want to know.

Whenever I blink, the image of Drew Yarrow's mouth on Mia's mouth flashes behind my closed lids, as if it's burned there. But, I'm encouraged to note, this isn't heartache I'm feeling.

It's cool, calm anger.

Drew and Mia—they're perfect for one another. Partners in hate.

We peel away from the police station, and Sharon brandishes her middle fingers to the SANG protesters as we leave them in our dust.

Chapter Nine: Falling Into Silver

"And you want to know what the *worst* part is, Court?"

I smile weakly at my sister as I hand over the cup of tea that I just brewed for her. It's one of Lare's teas, a blend called *Victor Hugo* — a complex black tea with notes of bergamot, lavender, and vanilla. Lare left a few packets of it on the kitchen counter with a handwritten note: *Sweets for the sweet.* Right away, I tucked the note into my jeans pocket; now I blush to imagine Lare writing it for me.

There was another note beside it, though, more hastily scribbled: Lare informing me that she'd been forced to return to her house due to "police business," begging me not to worry — and, anyway, it was good timing, she said, because Van Helsing was "overdue for his lunch."

To be honest, I breathed a sigh of relief when I came home to an empty house. I needed time to process my revelation about Mia, to figure out how to explain to Lare that I suspected my ex-girlfriend had vandalized her property.

"There's a *worst* part?" I ask Sharon

glumly, as I sit down in a chair with my own mug of tea.

Sharon is seated beside Marcus, who lies sprawled on my couch, his head resting against the throw pillow behind him. He stares owl-eyed up at the ceiling, as if he hasn't relaxed in days; his features are wan with exhaustion.

In contrast to her boyfriend's blank, silvered gaze, Sharon's eyes are wild, agitated. A little crazed. She keeps raking her hand through her black hair while crossing and uncrossing her black-stockinged legs.

She's in rage mode again.

"Of *course* there's a worst part. Because if there were enough *solid* evidence against her, Drew would *have* to be held—no bail, no get-out-of-jail free card. But there *isn't* enough evidence, so of course the police are going to let her go, as free as a bird." Sharon flaps her hands like wings. "Or...a harpy." She pauses to blow on her tea. Then a dark smile slides over her face. "But VampWatch will keep an eye on her. We're not going to let that lunatic kidnap anybody else."

"Sharon." My stomach tightens. I stare at my sister for a long moment, heedless of the steaming mug burning my fingertips. "What do you mean, *anybody else?*"

She lifts her chin, green eyes flashing. "I have reason to believe that Drew is *up* to something. I haven't figured it out yet. But when I do, the woman is going *down*."

I clear my throat, shifting uncomfortably. "Okay. Keeping an eye on Drew is important, but I think we all know that it's not enough. I mean, why *isn't* there enough evidence to hold her? You said that you saw her talking to Marta right before Marta was nearly kidnapped, right?"

"I did, but it's my word against hers. Drew denied ever speaking to Marta. And since there is, unfortunately, documented proof at the police station of my disgust toward SANG, my word doesn't count for all that much in this case. Too much bias. Plus," she adds, nudging Marcus with her hip, "I have a vampire fiance, and, as you know, the police don't look too kindly on our vampire friends." Sharon drinks down her tea in a single gulp and then shakes her head. "I just wish my eyes were equipped with surveillance cameras so that I could play back what I saw."

"You know, that's not the first time you've had that wish," says Marcus sleepily, flashing her a soft, suggestive smile.

And, despite everything, my sister smiles back at him.

There. Right *there*. *That's* how I know that Sharon and Marcus are meant to be together. No matter what's happening, no matter what type of predicament they find themselves in, good or bad, Marcus can always get my sister to soften, to step back, take a look at the bigger picture, and Sharon can do the same for him. Let's face it: it isn't every day that someone comes along who can soothe you in your darkest moments.

As I gaze at the two of them and sip my tea, my thoughts gradually drift toward Lare. I've only known Lare for a short while, true, but when I think about her, butterflies tickle my stomach, and I can't help but blush, smile, *glow*. There is, somehow, inexplicably, this bright, shining connection between the two of us, a bond that seems to grow stronger every time we interact.

The very first moment that I saw Valeria Máille, something stirred inside of me. Her spirit drew mine like a moth to the flame.

Watching Marcus and Sharon now, I wonder if I could ever have what they have, or if I'll make another wrong decision, like the one I made to trust Mia...

But then I think about Lare—her warmth, her passion, the way she makes me feel, the way she feels in my arms—and I don't wonder anymore.

"—right, Courtney?"

I glance up, surprised. "What?" Then I smile self-consciously. "Sorry, Sharon. I'm not used to going to rock concerts, and I didn't get much sleep last night. There's been...a lot of excitement around here. So, hey..." I straighten, rise, taking Sharon's empty teacup from her. "I think we're due for some of my famous spaghetti. Are you hungry?"

Sharon smiles fondly at me, then shakes her head. "I'm sorry, sis. It's not that I *don't* want your famous spaghetti. It's just been such a rough night. Day. Whatever. We didn't get a wink of sleep, and my stomach is too upset to digest anything right now. I think we're going to head home. I texted one of our roomies to come pick us up." She pats her pocket, where her phone resides. "So can I have a rain check on the p'sketti?"

"Sure."

Sharon and Marcus stand up, and then I hug my sister tightly, holding her as close as I can. "These are strange days, aren't they, kiddo?" I sigh. "The only thing we can do is keep fighting for what we believe in. And it'll all come up roses in the end."

"Dad used to say something like that," says Sharon, stepping back and offering me a soft smile. "You going to be okay? That graffiti next door looks pretty threatening."

Sharon and Marcus had noticed the vandalism on Lare's house front the moment we pulled into my driveway, so I had no choice but to tell them what I knew about the crime. I tried to downplay it, though; the two of them have enough to worry about.

"Yeah, I'm fine." My throat feels tight,

constricted. The word *fine* tastes like a lie. "Hey, Marcus, make sure she eats later, all right? And, Sharon—" I gaze into her eyes and shake my head. "Promise me that you'll get some rest."

"Scout's honor." She holds up her first two fingers with a wink.

Sharon and Marcus go outside to wait for their ride; a minute later, I hear a car horn honk, and Sharon shouts, "Later, Court!" before tires screech away.

The house, without them, feels oddly lonely.

I seek out Colette, who's claimed the back of the couch since our guests are gone. Her whiskers pucker in a stately kitty frown, as if to let me know that she hasn't forgiven me yet for the atrocity of inviting Van Helsing into our house.

I scratch her back and win a begrudging purr as I stare through the front window.

It's a lazy Saturday afternoon, and I have nothing planned, nothing to do. Normally, I cherish these sorts of slow, obligation-less days, but now, knowing that Lare is next door, I feel drawn to her. I long for her company.

And, more importantly than that, I'm worried about her. I haven't seen her since this morning; she's had to deal with prejudiced policemen all day long.

So I give Colette some wet food as a peace offering before I venture outdoors and trudge across the lawn. After a moment's hesitation, I knock on Lare's door.

And Lare answers on the second knock, as if she were expecting me.

She draws the door open, her silver-blue eyes softening as she gazes at my face. "Beautiful timing, as always." Lare's lips move into a warm, welcoming smile. Then she nods her head toward the road. "Would you like to take a walk with me? Van Helsing has been begging for one ever since we came home. And if he doesn't have his daily walk, he becomes a bit surly."

I glance at Van Helsing, sprawled on the hallway carpet as if he's superglued himself to it, his chin pillowed on his paws, his eyes closed. He's snoring softly.

I chuckle. "Surly? Really?"

"Well... Maybe not *surly* so much as fluffier in the belly." Lare plucks Van Helsing's leash from the hook by the doorway.

But even when he hears the jingle of the clip on the leash, Van Helsing remains, unmoving, on the floor. Still, a single ear flicks, and he opens his bleary eyes to stare up at his mistress.

"Come on, Helly," says Lare invitingly, waving the leash in front of his large nose. "Up for a constitutional?"

Van Helsing groans a little, as if to say, "Not really," but then he rises, shaking himself, jowls flapping against the side of his head. He ambles toward the door, reluctant but good-natured enough to humor us.

"That's my boy," says Lare, clipping the leash onto his collar. Then we all slip out into the afternoon sunshine.

I can't help side-eyeing the graffiti on the house as we move across Lare's lawn. Now that I suspect Mia committed the vandalism, I examine the blue penmanship carefully—and deduct, with a sinking sensation, that the handwriting *does* resemble Mia's wide, looping scrawl.

I tug nervously at the bun at the back of my neck and then shove my hands into my jeans pockets. "Lare," I begin, clearing my throat. "I...I may know—or at least, I have a good guess—still, it's just a guess—um, as to who *might* have spray-painted your house. I...think."

Lare raises a brow at me. "Okay. Who do you think it might have been? Anyone I know?" She guides Helly across the street, and I keep pace by her side.

"I..." I pause, drawing in a deep breath. "I think it was my ex, Mia Foster. She could have come here after our run-in at the concert. She knows where you live."

Lare is silent, tugging slow, heavy-footed Helly gently behind her. "Why do you think it was her?" she asks finally, staring ahead, working her jaw.

"A couple of things. When I picked Sharon and Marcus up from the station, Drew Yarrow was there, too." I wince. "And Mia was with her. With blue paint on her fingertips."

"Blue..." Lare considers this for a moment, silver eyes wide. Then she exhales and shakes her head of coppery waves. "It doesn't make sense. What does *I know what you did* mean? Mia doesn't know me, doesn't know..." But then she blinks, glances at me, her expression heartachingly sad. "Do you think Mia suspected that you and I..." Her voice trails off, but she doesn't need to finish her sentence. The truth is, I've been wondering the same thing.

By *I know what you did*, was Mia referring to Lare's relationship with me, insinuating that we were sleeping together?

I shake my head firmly, swallowing the lump in my throat. "It's possible. Though it does seem extreme, even for Mia. And *insanely* hypocritical." I kick a clump of loose dirt with the toe of my shoe. "But I guess Drew has brought out the extremist in her."

Lare walks quietly for several paces, hanging her head in a perfect imitation of the big, lumbering dog beside her. Helly's head is ducked down toward the sidewalk, as if he's more interested in the grass growing between the cracks than the expansive world shimmering around him.

"I didn't mean to complicate things for

you, Courtney."

I look to Lare in surprise. "Complicate?"

"Well, if it weren't for me—"

"No, Lare. No." I squint up into the sun, searching for the right words. "You haven't complicated anything. In fact, you've made things...very simple."

We pause, facing one another, and Lare reaches out for my hand.

"I'm a perfectionist, you know." I smile self-deprecatingly. "I try to fit everything in my life into neat little compartments—labeled, alphabetized. So, I have a job—check. A house—check. Never mind that I'm in danger of losing both of those things due to poor sales at the shop. At least I have them, right?"

Lare grazes her thumb over the back of my hand, listening.

I feel raw, vulnerable, and I never allowed myself to be raw and vulnerable with Mia, or any other romantic partner. But I'm learning that it's safe to reveal myself to Lare, to tell her the whole truth. So I take another shaky breath. And I go deeper, my voice cracking: "That's what you're *supposed* to have, a job and a house...and a partner. And so I had one of those, too. Mia."

Lare's eyes shift between crystal blue and mirrored silver, soft and shining as she gazes at me, as if she's trying to see all of me, down to my core.

"*Mia*," I whisper, flinching at the name, "didn't *pierce my soul* or make me feel *ardent* admiration or any Austenian thing like that. But I liked her company, was attracted to her. So I figured that must mean that I *loved* her..." I meet Lare's thoughtful stare. "I didn't, though."

"You didn't?" Her red brows arch.

"No. I didn't know what love felt like. I had no clue." I draw in a gulp of thick, humid air. "I wanted what Jane and Rochester have, that *string* thing—where they feel as if they're bound together by shared destiny, by mutual passion. I wanted it... But I didn't believe I'd ever find it." I stare into the depths of her silver eyes; they're bottomless, forever. I hold her hand tighter, screw up my courage, and say, "I didn't believe I'd find it, Lare. Until I met you."

Lare's eyes grow larger, gentler. They gleam like polished metal, glinting with flecks of sunlight. She lets go of my hand to curl her fingers around my waist. The distance between us closes; we're pressing against one another, holding one another. Then Lare leans forward and kisses me.

She kisses me as if we live in a world where hatred is a fairy tale.

She kisses me as if it's the first kiss that ever was, as if, by kissing each other, we're creating something new, something that will alter the universe as we know it.

It certainly alters me.

247

Lare breaks the kiss and drinks me in with silver eyes that are darkened with bare longing. I feel desire stoked within me, too, flaring as she grips my hip with her strong, practiced fingers.

Then Lare raises a single brow. She doesn't speak, only inclines her head toward our block, with an obvious question in her eyes. I nod, heart throbbing in my chest, and I grip her hand tightly. Together we begin to stroll back toward my house, Helly just behind us, tail wagging now that his walk, at last, is done.

I unlock the door, and slowly, carefully, as if I have all the time in the world, I set up Van Helsing—with water, a blanket, the stuffed cat toy that Colette never acknowledges—in the guest bedroom again. I double-check, before I close the door, that Colette is occupied elsewhere, and I'm relieved to find her stalking a shadow in the hallway. "Have a nice nap, Helly," I whisper.

When I glance down at my hand on the doorknob, I realize that it's shaking.

I think every atom in my whole body is shaking.

When I summon up the courage to walk to the threshold of my bedroom, I draw in a quavery breath.

Lare is seated, legs crossed, on the edge of my bed. She's leaning back on her hands, and her head is tilted to one side; red waves spill over her shoulder. The lights are off, but sunshine filters through the filmy curtains, illuminating the planes of her face, the soft curve of her breasts. I notice, with a flush of heat, that the buttons of her lavender shirt are already undone, top to bottom...

I cross the space between us, and slowly, reverently, I kneel down in front of her. When she gazes at me, my breath catches: the deep, dark, silver-blue of her eyes pins me in place. Waves of desire shudder throughout my body as I brush my hand over her calf, then curl my fingers around her leg and trace gently, softly, up into the warm curve of her knee, along her thigh. Lare exhales and opens her legs in one smooth, silent motion.

I move between her legs and angle my face up, drawing one arm around her neck, pulling her mouth down toward me. I taste her, kiss her, find her wanting me just as much as I want her. Her tongue moves past my lips, seeking.

Lare moans as my hand finds the button of her jeans, as I undo it and peel down her zipper. She shimmies, and I tug her pants over her rear, her legs, her ankles, discarding them in a messy pile at the foot of the bed.

I sit back on my heels then, hooking my fingers beneath the hem of my t-shirt. I pull it over my head, my loosened hair falling against bare shoulders, causing me to shiver. Lare stares at me with those all-seeing eyes, eyes that reflect me as I lick my lips and unclasp my bra.

And then she's here, right here: she slides off of the bed, eases on top of me. She removes my bra with expert grace as she kisses me hard, tossing the confection of lace and silk aside. I groan as her hand finds my left nipple. She squeezes my breast, and she's between my legs, but I'm still wearing my jeans...so she teases me, taunts me, supernaturally resisting the urge to press her hips against my own. She straddles me, then, staring down at me with a toothy, mischievous grin as she shrugs out of her own shirt, letting it slide over her shoulders.

I reach up, brushing my fingers against her soft curls, but Lare interrupts, taking my wrists and pressing them down gently into the carpeting on either side of my head.

She arches over me, and her hair drifts over my face in a perfumed cloud: lilies, sugar, sex. I feel her teeth around my nipple and cry out, biting my lip as *she* bites down, tugging, tugging. I bend my head back; I can feel her smiling against my skin.

She traces a pattern of kisses, of gentle, lovely bites, back and forth between my breasts, leaving a wet trail between them. She lets go of my wrists, kissing lower and lower, trailing her tongue lower and lower, until she laves against the indentation of my belly button. I gasp as her fingers curl under the hem of my panties, tugging them down over my hips with an insistent pull.

Lare, too, removes her bra, her bottoms, her actions desperate, evidence of need. She can't wait anymore. *I* can't wait anymore. When our naked bodies collide, I hiss out in pleasure as I spread my legs, wrapping them around her so that my center and hers make exquisite contact. She presses down, and I can feel how wet I am against her, and when she moves, rising and falling in an undulating rhythm, my pulse pounds through me, concentrating on that perfect place where our bodies blend and burn.

She pauses, panting, her mouth open, her eyes as dark as night. I shiver beneath her, glimpsing the power, the raw desire in her stare. Lare reaches down with a slow hand, prolonging her desperation, my desperation. I hold myself as still as possible, but I tremble with anticipation. And then her nails are against my stomach, seeking down, down, until she finds and claims my wet curve. Jolted, I spread my legs further, aching, asking. Lare smiles into my shoulder, and I can feel the points of her teeth against my skin.

I breathe out in a moan, feeling my wetness accommodate her fingers, feeling my body shift and respond to her. Lare presses her mouth to my ear, kisses me softly there as she finds a new rhythm, curling her fingers inside of me, pressing her thumb to my clit with delicious pressure.

I cry out her name as the rhythm intensifies, as the length of her body, of my body, meld into one being. I know where she is, where every inch of her is in relation to me, even though my eyes are closed, even though my head is thrown back, even though I'm floating in a perfect, incandescent darkness.

Then I feel her teeth at my neck again.

And in this moment, I realize something shocking: I would let her drink from me.

I have lain myself bare to her in every way, and I would let her join me in every way if she wanted to. But she doesn't want to. I feel that truth in my bones. Lare is a vampire, yes, but she's dedicated her career to finding an alternative to blood, to raising her species up, to trying to make things *better*. For everyone.

I don't know how other vampires make love to humans—my sister, typically a fount of information, is close-lipped about her sex life with Marcus—but I do know that this experience is unlike any I've ever had before. I can feel the hardness of her teeth at my neck as she curls and curves her fingers inside of me, flicking her thumb in a maddening cadence as I wrap my arms around her shoulders, tighten my legs at her waist, as the two of us move together, merge together.

When the orgasm comes, I see stars, bright points of light that explode in my vision, dissolving everything else, all that I am. The build-up of pressure, that perfect, sweet release, sweeps through my muscles in undulating waves of pleasure. I feel open, discovered...undone.

Lare holds me tightly, teasing wave after wave out of me until I'm trembling, weak, until I arc past the edge and feel too much sensation, too much grandeur...

And then, intuitively, she stops. As if she knows me, inside and out. As if she can read me like a well-loved book.

She trails her wet fingers up my leg slowly, slowly, along my side, shaping them to the curve of my hip, tracing a shining line over my skin as I pant beneath her, as I try to catch my breath. Arching over me, Lare brushes her lips against mine.

I return her kiss—gently, softly. I just want to taste her, marvel at her. She presses little kisses to my jaw, the hollow under my chin, my neck, the curve behind my ear, and then she moves down my neck to my clavicle, my sternum, my breasts, kissing me over and over again as I sigh, in wonder, beneath her.

She says, "You move like all the right words," her French accent pronounced, her words low, thick. I wrap my fingers in her hair, letting the caress of her satin curls tease my skin. "You move like the perfect line in a book," she goes on, whispering, her head tilted to the side as she rests her chin on my breast, pressing a kiss to my peaked nipple. "I want to learn your every line," she tells me then, her voice fervent. "I want to memorize every line of you."

I sit up on my elbows, strength and need and want surging back into me.

I don't say anything, because I can think of nothing to say. Instead, I kiss her hard, aching for her all over again.

Breathless, I crawl on top of Lare, pressing my body against hers. Beneath me, her red hair fans out around her head like sunbeams, and when I bend down to kiss her, I dwell in her warmth: the warmth of her skin, of her red mouth, of her curves.

We fit together like two gold-gilt pages in a rare, secret book.

Chapter Ten: Trust Me

I wake to the toe-curling sensation of a warm mouth pressed to the slope of my neck. My eyes flutter open, and my body curves toward Lare's, as if by deep instinct.

"Courtney?" Lare whispers, her voice low and soft in my ear. "I'm sorry. I hate to wake you. But I have to go and wanted to say goodbye."

"Oh..." I blink, then sit up on my elbows, glancing at the bedside clock. It's half past four in the morning and still pitch dark outside. The light from the hallway casts Lare's face in shadows. "What's wrong?"

"Don't worry," she tells me soothingly, pressing a kiss to my forehead. "I got a page from work. There's been an emergency."

"What? Another—"

"They just need my help with something. So I told them I'm come in."

I wrap my fingers around the collar of her white shirt, already buttoned up. She's fully dressed, and wet curls drape over her shoulders, as if she just took a shower. Leaning down again, she presses her mouth to the tender place where my neck meets my shoulder.

I swallow, holding tightly to her. "Just...be careful," I breathe into her ear.

We made love Saturday evening and spent a languorous Sunday in bed, rising occasionally to eat or drink or tend to Helly and Colette. Decadent hours, and a sublime shiver of pleasure moves through me as I realize that this is only the beginning. The beginning of many, many hours together, learning the languages of our bodies and our hearts.

Lare stares down at me with soft, shimmering blue eyes and an intimate smile. A smile meant only for me. "I'll be careful," she promises, touching her lips to my bare shoulder. "And don't forget that today is Monday, my dear bookseller," she teases. "I have to admit, I lost track of time this weekend... And it was lovely." Her gaze pierces me. "So lovely. Like a dream."

I offer her a lopsided smile. "And now we have to return to the real world."

"Ah, but the real world is more beautiful now — don't you think?"

"Yes," I agree, pulling her close.

She presses her mouth against mine, but the kiss is too short: sighing, she pulls away regretfully. "I'll see you after work, *ma chere*," she says, and then she moves through the open bedroom door. The hallway light filters through the copper strands of Lare's hair, and my heart rises as she turns, silhouetted, to give me one last glance of farewell, her hand lifted, her mouth curved into a secret smile.

And then she's gone.

I ache when I hear the front door close, when I hear Lare's engine start up outside.

I miss her already.

Funny how everything can change so quickly, so unexpectedly. I've always been a planner—but how could I have planned for this? Impossible, because I couldn't have imagined such soul-deep happiness in my wildest dreams.

I sit up, stretching. Every inch of my body is sore, swollen with kisses. I lean forward, arms around my knees, smiling to myself.

Colette jumps onto the bed and glances at me with a smug expression, her whiskers pointed toward me as if to say, in a snooty accent, "You've lost your head, young lady." I laugh lightly as I scratch her behind the ears. Then, with a resigned sigh, I stand up and prepare for the day—starting with a long, hot shower.

Once I've dressed, eaten breakfast, and fed Colette, I step outside to face down my car with a doubtful frown. But, weirdly enough, Colonel Mustard starts without complaint, ready and rumbling. Even my old clunker is in a good mood today.

Weirder still, as I drive to work, I catch myself whistling.

Whistling? I can't remember the last time I

whistled...

Have I *ever* whistled? I chuckle to myself. Apparently, Lare triggered a dormant urge to whistle inside of me.

Or maybe I've just never felt this happy before.

When I walk into Banks' Books, warm vanilla latte in hand, I'm greeted by a long-armed wave from Azure, who's shelving books in the history section. Her military-style boots are planted firmly on the ladder. I notice that her earrings are mismatched, and her purple mohawk looks a little squished—but Azure traditionally loathes Mondays.

"How's it hangin', boss?" she calls out, casting a half-glance in my direction.

Then she stops, freezing in place, and drops the book in her hand. Her brow is furrowed, her head tilted to one side, like a dog tuning in to a distant, high-pitched sound. "*Wait* a second," she exclaims, hopping over the rungs to land squarely on the floor. She picks up the dropped book and brandishes it at me. "Courtney...were you just *whistling?*"

I stow my purse under the front desk and bat my eyes innocently. "Is whistling a crime?"

"No, but..." Her mouth hangs open for a long moment, a *comically* long moment. I bite my lip to hold back my laughter. Then her face lights up like a Christmas tree—that's been set on fire. "Wait a *second!*" she says again, holding up a finger in perfect imitation of the cover illustration of a Sherlock Holmes book we have in stock. "Something outrageously *outrageous* must have happened to make you so damn cheerful on a Monday morning."

She taps her boot on the floor, squinting at me, considering the case. Then her eyes fly wide open; she leans toward me, mouth smirking in triumph. "You broke up with Mia, didn't you?" Her voice is low, conspiratorial, like a kid asking her parent if she's going to get a puppy for her birthday.

I stare her down and tilt up my chin. "Yes," I say, hands on my hips. "Good work, detective."

Azure leaps around like a bunny on a trampoline, shooting her hand into the air to give me a high five. "That's awesome. I mean, *seriously* awesome. God, that's so awesome. I mean...*awesome.*" She pauses to bite her lip, studying my expression. Then she tries—and fails—to look penitent. "Sorry, sorry, I know this is a big deal for you. It's hard to break up with anyone, even a bi—I mean, a *person* like Mia. I should try to be more—"

"Hey, throw a party, if you want." I smile weakly. "I'm struggling with some issues related to Mia right now, but none of them has to do with our breaking up. Mia...really isn't who I thought she was. I don't even think she's who *she* thought she was," I mutter, raking a hand through my hair.

Then I lean forward on the desk. I'm too excited not to talk about it, and Azure, as my best friend, deserves to be in the loop. "Guess what else happened..."

"Cripes!" Azure places the back of her hand on her forehead, as if she has a fever. "Courtney Banks, playing guessing games? Am I hearing things? Are you feeling all right?" She moves her hand to *my* forehead. "You are kind of warm. Kind of...blushing. God, it's like you've got a crush or something. Now, I *know* you don't have a crush on me, so..." Azure trails off as my smiles deepens, and then she's grabbing my hands and squealing, "Oh, my God! Oh, my God! *Courtney Banks, did you sleep with the vampire?*"

I don't have to answer her: my head-duck and deepening blush give me away.

"Way to go, bookworm!" Azure picks up my limp arm to give me another high five. "This is ah-*may*-zing. You have to tell me all about it. I mean, right *now*. We should close the store for the day, make some popcorn, and then let's go sit in your office so you can spill every sordid, juicy detail—"

"Breathe, Azure," I laugh.

Then she grabs me by the shoulders and draws me close for a rib-crushing hug. "I have a good feeling about this, Court." When she lets me go, she gazes deeply into my eyes, her features uncharacteristically serious. "You look different, you know. I've never seen you so—I don't know—*bright*. So happy." Her voice is low, awed.

I smile. "Thank you. But we have other things to talk about besides my weekend. Azure, you were *incredible* on stage—" I begin, but my phone starts to vibrate inside of my purse. "Sorry." I sigh, snap open the purse, and then fish out my cell. "How many phone numbers did you get up there, anyway?" I ask Azure, grinning, as I select my text messages folder. "And how many *bras*?"

"Oh, you know, a *lot*," says Azure, with a small shrug and a wicked smile.

Laughing, I glance down at my screen—and the world falls out from under me.

The text is from Mia.

Baby, it reads, *look...I left the group. I'm done with Drew. She was so wrong, and I'm so sorry. Please come to my apartment? I want to talk, part on friendly terms. Don't let us end like this. I know I messed up. I just want to apologize in person. I really do love you, Courtney.*

Without a doubt, the longest text Mia has ever sent me. And the most heartfelt. Her previous messages were something along the lines of, *Sex, your place?* Or, *In the mood for Italian or Chinese?*

As I stare down at the phone, I know, without question, that I'd rather walk over burning coals than go to Mia's apartment. Still, I'm surprised. Surprised that Mia broke up with Drew, especially after I saw her hanging off of Drew's arm like one of those fish who suction-cup their mouths to the belly of a shark.

I grimace, sliding the phone back into my purse. What *probably* happened is that Drew broke up with Mia, and now Mia realizes that all of the things she did to me were pretty rotten. She just wants to clear her conscience.

Be that as it may...I hate the way we ended things. And I, too, want some closure. More than that, I want answers. I want to know why Mia cheated on me, and I want to ask her if she vandalized Lare's house. Maybe her fingers were blue because she'd just eaten blueberries, or been to a painting class, or—I don't know—arm-wrestled a Smurf. Unlikely possibilities, granted. Mia told me once that she hates blueberries, and she's never been into art of any kind, aside from writing. As for Smurfs... Well, to the best of my knowledge, they're fictional creatures. But, admittedly, I've been proven wrong before.

Regardless, I need to know the truth—for Lare's sake. And for mine.

Mia's apartment is a ten-minute drive away. I'll take my lunch break early, and then I'll have a built-in, and honest, escape plan, because I'll have to return to the shop within half an hour. Just one half hour in my ex-girlfriend's presence, and then I'll be able to get on with the rest of my life.

My life with Lare.

I straighten my shoulders and flick my gaze to Azure, who's watching me with narrowed eyes.

"All right there, chickadee?" she asks, concerned. "You look like you just saw a ghost. In text form."

"It's just some...business," I say evasively, clearing my throat and placing the phone on the desk, face down.

I know that, if I tell Azure where I'm planning to go, who I'm planning to see, she'll try to talk me out of it. She might even go so far as to lock the shop door and hide the key. She'd say, *Courtney, don't walk back into the fire...* And the thing is, she'd be right. But this is an opportunity to press Mia for information, information that I have no other way to obtain.

So, shortly before noon, I tell Azure, "Hey, I'm going to take my lunch break early. Something came up—"

"Off for a quickie, are you?" she winks, as she pages through a Victorian etiquette book.

"Something like that." I sling my purse over my shoulder and leave the store without another word, dread sitting like a rock in the pit of my stomach.

Mia's apartment is a tiny studio located in a rundown neighborhood of Cincinnati. She could afford better, but—as she told me once—she spends so little time at her place, she doesn't see any sense in wasting her hard-earned money on a larger apartment.

I jog up the two flights of stairs to her floor and knock on the paint-flaking door, heart Jackhammering in my chest. Given Mia's text message, I expect an effusive welcome, but I'm greeted by a distracted, listless Mia who gestures me inside without a greeting, without a hug.

An odd feeling of foreboding pricks at my nerves, but I walk in, anyway, moving into the small living room.

Exhaling heavily, I glance around. The place looks messy, as always, but now I feel as if I'm seeing it through new eyes. There are *things* everywhere—on her counter, her sofa, her desk. Discordant, mismatched things with no connection to one another, or to her. Classical CDs, books about zookeeping, a pair of roller skates that are scuffed at the toes. I lick my lips, shaking my head. Mia's lived a hundred lives—and none of them has ever stuck.

Resting on the never-used kitchen table are the weights for a Zumba class that Mia took—because she thought the instructor was "hotter than the sun." There on the kitchen counter is a stack of beginner's piano music from that time she decided to try out piano lessons — because the teacher was a gorgeous redhead in her late twenties who, and I quote, gave Mia some "hands-on training." There on her couch is the sword and shield from that stint in the Society for Creative Anachronism; there on the floor is a video game console she doesn't play anymore, bought to impress "that cute chick at the video game store."

And there on the bar stool is the copy of *Jane Eyre* I gave her when we first started dating. It's nearly hidden beneath a pile of laundry, but I can make out its red leather cover. She told me she'd read it, loved it, but now I'm not so sure. I'm not sure that anything she told me was true.

And I wonder, with the clarity born from time, distance, and pain, how many women Mia slept with while she was in a relationship with me. She promised that she never cheated, but Mia is, if nothing else, desperate to belong. To be connected — if only in the fleeting way that a one-night stand connects you to someone. She wants to be a part of the lives of women who are more assured of who they are than Mia could ever dream of being. It's a different form of vampirism — an insidious form, draining people of their confidence, their identities, rather than their blood.

I set my jaw and take in the woman before me. She looks like a stranger: sad, waif-like, wearing a beat-up, too-big black hoodie, twisting her hands together, her face frightfully pale. I don't think she's been getting enough sleep. Or *any* sleep.

I take a deep breath, and I'm about to speak when Mia lifts up her hand, tries a very fake, too-bright, brittle smile on for size. "Can I get you some water?" she asks me, voice wavering.

"No, thank you." I raise a brow as I watch Mia pace over to the couch, and then—at the last moment—decide that she doesn't want to sit, after all. She turns back toward me and shrugs, sighs. But she says nothing. God, she won't even look me in the eyes.

"Um, you said you wanted to talk to me?" I prompt her when she does the same thing with the corner chair: she walks up to it, as if she intends to sit down, and then she veers away, standing behind it, resting her hand on the chair back. A hand that, I can't help but notice, is shaking like a leaf in the wind.

Okay, she's acting...weird. Frazzled. Upset. As Mia turns to, reluctantly, face me again, I realize that she isn't really pale; she caked on a large amount of foundation. But where the foundation has smeared, her skin reveals itself to be a raw, bright red beneath.

Pretty sure she's trying to hide the fact that she's been crying...

"Are you all right?" I ask her, heavily, tiredly, figuring that my deduction was spot on:

Drew *did* break up with Mia, not vice versa, which means this will likely be a very messy conversation. I'm not the coolest, cleverest, or prettiest woman in the world—far from it—but if there's something Mia can't endure, it's being alone. And if Drew broke up with her, she's going to ask me to forgive her, to come back to her, and I don't think I have the strength for that right now...

"Look, Courtney," says Mia, voice catching. Her brown eyes roam all over the small room, glancing everywhere that I am not. Finally, they dart toward the door and linger there for a long moment. "Look," she begins again, with something like desperation in her tone. She steps forward, and then she takes my right wrist in her cold fingers, squeezing it tightly in her hand.

"I'm *sorry*," she whispers, as a tear squeezes out of her eye.

I'm stunned, taken aback. This apology is *sincere*.

Suddenly, the door to the apartment opens behind us; I turn, surprised.

But my surprise quickly gives way to shock as I see Drew Yarrow moving into the room, high heels sinking into the stained carpeting. Wearing a tight black pencil skirt and a lacy black blouse, she looks chic, out of place.

She wrinkles her nose, peering around the apartment with an upraised chin. I can tell that she hasn't been here before, and revulsion is written plainly on her scary-lovely face.

When her gaze shifts to Mia and me at last, she smiles.

But it's the smile of a predator who's about to catch one hell of a meal.

My stomach twists in fear.

Drew turns slightly then, glancing over her shoulder. "Come on in," she says quietly, and several people begin to fill the small space—men and women dressed in black clothing, their hair hidden beneath black baseball caps, as if they're part of a SWAT team. I recognize one or two of them from the police station. I'm surrounded by a crowd of SANG fanatics.

"Courtney, I'm sorry," Mia chokes out, and when I look to her, I see that she's crying, really crying...

And that's when a tight piece of cloth swoops over my eyes, followed immediately by another over my mouth.

Oh.

My fight or flight instincts kick in: I'm throwing my weight forward, punching, clawing, but someone with strong hands restrains my arms, tying them roughly behind my back. I yell against the gag in my mouth, but then a wide piece of tape is fastened over the cloth, silencing me. I feel like I'm going to suffocate.

My legs are tied together at the ankles,

and then I tip over, stiffening, waiting for impact with the floor, but the couch catches me. I bounce on the cushions, taking in a deep breath through my nose, trying to still my erratic heartbeat.

What the *hell* is this?

"Good work," Drew says sharply. "Get her ready to transport, team."

I'm in the air, then, supported by several pairs of hands, toted down the back stairs like a worn-out futon. Either no one sees the parade of black-clad people carrying me—or no one dares to get in the way. Light and dark alternate behind the blindfold, and finally I'm rolled hard onto what feels like the thinly carpeted floor of a vehicle.

"Watch her head," someone says, and then my head is pushed down. There's a thump above me, followed by a harsh *click*.

Then, only darkness.

I think I'm in the trunk of a car.

My suspicion is confirmed when the car starts up; I can feel gears rumbling beneath me. The car takes off hard, tires screeching, and I'm thrown against the back wall of the trunk with a sickening *thud*.

An eternity passes. At least, that's what it feels like to me. And time is relative, right? Although I was afraid when all of this began, I've had a few eons to consider what's happening to me, and the fear has evaporated, now replaced by something darker, something far more powerful.

I'm *pissed*. Livid. I feel like the Incredible Hulk, angry enough to burst out of my confines and *smash* everything in sight. But, unfortunately, when I struggle with the knot at my wrists, I only succeed in making it tighter.

Mia set this up, inviting me to her apartment under the false pretense of *closure*. I keep seeing Drew's perfect, ugly mask in my mind's eye, keep hearing her low, controlled voice bark out orders to her minions. I never believed in *evil* – textbook definition *evil* – until today, until I saw the nothingness behind Drew Yarrow's eyes.

I bask in anger, a white-bright fury, because it keeps the encroaching panic at bay.

Mia kept saying she was sorry, and she *had* seemed to be genuinely sorry, but that hadn't stopped her from going along with this vendetta. And there's more coming. Obviously, they have some sort of *plan* for me. I wrack my brain to figure out the reason SANG chose to kidnap me, and the one I keep circling back to is...Lare.

They've kidnapped me because of Lare.

Because Mia hates Lare, and Lare is a vampire.

And that means Lare is in danger, too.

No. Over my dead body.

I wriggle against the ropes, wincing as my

skin burns. Then I growl in frustration, shutting my eyes against the blindfold, resting with my nose scratching against the trunk mat; it smells of chemicals, windshield wiper fluid.

Okay, so brute strength has never been my strong point, Hulk inclinations notwithstanding.

I'm a thinker.

I have to *think* my way out of this.

When the car stops and the trunk is opened, the quality of light changes. It's still daytime. I'm moved quickly, two hands in my armpits and a big arm around my knees, into something that darkens the sun. A building, I assume, and my hunch is proven correct when I hear the hollow sound of a metal door closing behind us.

That door closing...

A final, terrible sound.

I'm tossed unceremoniously onto a chair—it's cold against my hot skin—and something happens with my ropes: a moment later, I realize I've been knotted to the chair. That's when my blindfold is yanked off of of my face, taking several hanks of hair along with it.

I stare forward, waiting for my eyes to adjust to the dimness of the room. Then I glance sideways and try to take everything in... My breath catches in my throat.

I'm sitting on the last chair in a row of three metal chairs. The other two are occupied by men. One of the men is older, with graying hair and a receding hairline, glasses sitting askew on his nose. The other one is younger, red hair and a beard. He's seated closest to me.

Both of the men are tied to their chairs and gagged, just like I am.

And, judging by their silverless eyes, both of the men are human.

They look ragged, drained. As if they've been here for a while. They aren't new arrivals, like me.

All at once, my blood runs cold.

I think I know who these people are.

I think they're the kidnap victims from Give Life Technologies.

Oh, my God... Drew Yarrow *is* responsible for the kidnappings, just like my sister suspected. But *why*? Why kidnap humans, when it's vampires that she detests?

"Is she here yet?" Drew snaps, drawing my attention. She's standing a few feet away from me, directing the question to a man in black whose straight, deferential posture suggests military experience.

"Not yet. She will arrive momentarily," he answers, staring straight ahead.

Drew stalks past him, glancing down at me with thinly veiled contempt. She stabs a bright-red nail into my shoulder.

"I want you to know," she says, voice sickeningly sweet, "that all of this was *your* fault."

My heart rate skyrockets. I swallow against the gag.

Behind my back, I hear the metal door open and close again—followed by the sound of footsteps on the concrete floor.

I turn around slightly, craning my neck as I struggle against the ropes, and I see two people standing still beneath the warehouse rafters: a big, burly guy wearing a SANG jacket—and Lare.

Lare takes a step forward, walking freely, her chin tilted up, but she's gagged, and it's obvious that her hands are bound behind her back. She's wearing the same clothes she was wearing in the wee hours of the morning, when everything was normal, good—better than good. How is this possible? How is this real?

Lare's white button-down shirt now has dark smudges on it, and there's a stiffness in her gait.

She stares at me, shoulders rising, while Drew folds her hands together and rolls her soulless eyes. "Ah, the lovers reunited." She smiles without mirth.

Mia appears, then, in the corner of my eye—she wasn't here just a moment ago—and I glare at her in disgust. But Mia doesn't feel my loathing, because Mia isn't looking at me. She only has eyes for Drew. In her black ballet flats—shoes I've seen a hundred times before, lying on the floor of my entryway—she scampers up to Drew's side and hangs onto her arm, nuzzling her face against the woman's shoulder.

I'm going to be sick.

"Now that everybody's here, we're ready to go, right?" Mia asks Drew in a low, excited voice. Drew gazes sidelong at her and nods tightly. "Wonderful, wonderful," says Mia, stepping away from Drew and approaching me, sinking down onto her heels with wide eyes. "I really *am* sorry about all of this, Courtney." She grimaces, but her dark eyes are shining with a deranged, exuberant light. "You've got to understand," she goes on, speaking slowly, as if she's explaining something complicated to a small child, "we only want to prove what we've always known, that vampires are a poison to society."

My chest rises and falls in a furious sigh.

"Vampires will ruin things for themselves eventually. They're animals, after all, destructive animals with destructive needs." Mia shakes her head. "But SANG doesn't want to wait for the vampires to kill innocent humans. Don't you understand? We're saving human lives by doing this! Anyway," she tells me, smiling softly, "we picked Lare because of you. We hadn't had anyone specific in mind before. We were just going to grab the first vampire we found."

Her mouth twists into a frown. "But I

couldn't *stand* the thought of you being touched by that...*thing.*" Her eyes glow, bright and dangerous. "So we worked together, Drew and I, to make certain that it was Lare who was framed. I even spray-painted her house," says Mia, lifting her fingers so that I can see the faint hint of blue on them now. "You shouldn't have let yourself be manipulated by that monster, Courtney. I'm worried about you." She holds my gaze, peering intently—as if concerned—at my face.

I want to scream. I want to slap her across the room. But I can't do anything besides sit here, nostrils flaring as I try to take deep, even breaths to prevent myself from fainting.

So. SANG was planning to frame a vampire for these kidnappings all along, in order to hurt the pro-vampire cause, to turn public opinion against vampirekind, in general.

I know what you did—Mia spray-painted those words on Lare's house to backup their evolving plan, to insinuate that Lare was guilty.

And they only chose Lare as their scapegoat because of *me.* That's what Drew meant when she said it was all my fault.

I close my eyes so that I can't see Mia, can't see Drew. I'm repulsed by the sight of both of them. I inhale several short, quick breaths, and then, begrudgingly, I open my eyes again.

"Good girl." Drew pets Mia's head condescendingly. "Why don't you go into the back room—our little room—now?" she purrs, offering Mia a hand to help her rise; then she wraps her arms around Mia's narrow waist. "I'll join you in just a minute. I want to show you how proud of you I am," she says, with an indulgent smile. She kisses Mia hard, and when Mia turns around to leave, Drew smacks Mia on the bottom.

I suck in an annoyed breath through my nose.

"That goes for the rest of you, too," says Drew, striding forward and circling Lare, head held high, back arrow straight. "You've done good work," Drew assures her minions. "Go to the break room and start celebrating. I'll catch up with you shortly to debrief. There's one last thing I have to do."

"Boss?" says the guy with the military manners. He shifts his gaze to Lare uncertainly, sizing her up. "Do you need my help?"

"Did I ask for your help? Do as you're told." Drew claps her hands and gives the man a deadly smile. He hesitates, then nods, and the rest of the people in the room shuffle toward the back of the warehouse, disappearing through a gray-painted door. As they filter out, I hear someone whistling a tune that's vaguely familiar. It's slick, catchy...

David. That's the tune that David whistled in the bookstore.

I can't help wondering: how many people

in Cincinnati are—secretly or not-so-secretly—supporters of SANG?

No...I don't want to know. I don't want to know that people I see every day-- friendly, well-adjusted people—can harbor such seething, unfounded hatred within them.

"Valeria Máille," pronounces Drew, who is now the only unrestrained person in the cavernous room. "That is your proper name, isn't it?"

Lare says nothing; the gag is still in place. But she lifts her chin a little higher, staring straight ahead as she tenses her jaw.

"I have reason to believe that there's someone in this room that you care for a great deal." Drew flicks a bland glance in my direction. "So I think you'll do as I ask, in order to assure her safety. Am I correct in my assumption?"

Lare looks to me, her eyes shining with pain. She draws in a deep breath, nostrils flaring. Then she regards Drew again, and her expression changes: the silver in her eyes deepens, darkens, as if with a warning.

Drew chuckles softly, matching Lare's stare. "I seem to have struck a nerve with you, *animal*," she says thoughtfully, tilting her blonde head. "I should tell you, though, that I only asked that question out of curiosity. Because, no matter what you do, you will not be able to help this woman, just as you will not be able to help these men. You see, they—and you—are about to die."

My heart plummets, and the man beside me begins to whimper.

I watch Lare's shoulders rise; I can see her brow furrowed in concentration. A drop of sweat rolls over her forehead as her muscles strain.

She's trying to get out of the ropes restraining her wrists.

"A valiant attempt, but you can't escape," says Drew, noticing Lare's efforts without missing a beat. "Besides, I'm just as fast and strong as you are." She slips behind Lare's back and flicks her nails across her throat. "Let's get this over with, shall we?" And with that, she rips the tape off of Lare's face and removes the gag.

Lare exhales heavily, breathing hard.

Then I stare, perplexed, as Drew puts her fingers into Lare's mouth and drags something out of it.

What. The Hell?

It looks like...a dental mold.

Lare flexes her jaw, exhausted, beaten. There are purple bruises around her mouth. My soul aches for her, pines for her. I just want to hold her, kiss her, one last time...

All business now, Drew crosses the room to approach a crate, still holding the piece of silicon or plastic that she extracted from Lare's mouth in her clawed hand.

Moving on silent feet, Lare positions herself next to me, flicking her gaze to the men in the two other chairs, her face soft with compassion, gray with sorrow. "I'm so sorry, George, Daniel," she whispers. "I'm...so sorry."

She sinks down beside me, kneeling on one knee, her shoulders straining forward because of her bound wrists. "Courtney," she tells me, the word thick with emotion, "we're going to get out of this alive. I promise you that." Her voice, though weak, is emphatic, passionate. "I've just got to—"

"All done!" says Drew, whirling around with a wicked smile. She stalks back toward us, making a show of hiding something behind her back. Her glassy eyes flick between Lare and me as her mouth curves into a deep, disapproving frown. "The time for sentiment has passed, I'm afraid."

"What are you going to do?" Lare asks heavily, rising up.

That's when I see what, exactly, that goon used to restrain Lare's wrists: zip ties. Zip ties are impossible to struggle out of; they're too thick, too strong, too sturdy to break with bare hands.

And yet... I watch as Lare's fingers worry at the thick plastic, slicing into it, bit by bit, with her sharp nails. Vampire strength? The plastic is slowly giving way, but Lare isn't quite free yet.

"I'm going to do something I've *longed* to do for my entire *life*." Drew takes her hands from behind her back and lifts them toward her mouth. She seems to be affixing something...to her *teeth*?

"I'm a completionist, Lare. I don't like to do anything halfway," Drew offers conversationally, though her words are thick, muffled, as she continues to fiddle with her mouth. "I have to make the authorities believe that a *vampire* kidnapped and killed these three poor, innocent humans. Before SANG came in to witness the atrocity, of course." Drew parts her lips to bare a wicked smile...

I pale.

She's wearing fangs.

"Of course, if I intend to frame *you* for this crime, it can't be just *any* vampire who commits the murders. When the police examine the bodies, they must find *your* saliva and *your* distinctive teeth marks on the victims' necks." Drew pauses to smile toothily at each of us, in turn. "Come on, admit it. You're impressed by my attention to detail, aren't you? Creating a mold of your mouth was a stroke of brilliance."

Lare stares at Drew with round, silver eyes. "What will you do with me after you kill everyone here?" she asks, voice low.

"Kill you, too, naturally." Drew smiles disbelievingly and shakes her head, as if the answer to Lare's question were obvious. "What else *could* I do? You don't deserve to live."

"And why is that?" asks Lare gruffly, lifting her chin. She's stalling. Her fingers move back and forth, tugging gently at the zip ties. Gently, so as not to give herself away.

I hold my breath, watching the plastic tear.

"Because you're a monster," Drew says simply. "And if movies have taught us anything, it's that monsters are dangerous and must be exterminated."

"Mm." Lare shrugs her shoulders—to get a better grip on the zip ties. "I just need to know one thing before I die."

"Yes?"

"Why do you hate vampires so much? You're a smart woman. You must have a *reason* for all of this hatred, all of this effort you've put into the cause. Tell me—what did we ever do to you?" Lare asks mildly, as if she's genuinely curious.

Drew's unsettling eyes narrow. "That, beast, is none of your business."

"Okay. But the thing is," says Lare, standing tall, her head tilted to one side, red hair falling over her shoulder, "there's...something about you. The first time I saw your face on TV, you seemed familiar."

"Shut up."

"And I thought to myself," Lare continues, commanding Drew's gaze, *"That woman is full of hate*. And the thing that we hate the most is often to be found within ourselves."

Drew steps forward, inhaling sharply.

"You're a vampire, aren't you?" Lare says simply. "You're one of us. And you *hate* yourself for it."

I gasp against my gag. *What?* Drew Yarrow, a vampire? No. No, it's not *possible*. Is it?

Drew has yet to confirm or deny Lare's accusation. She's frozen; her eyes are clamped onto Lare's face, as if she's physically unable to look away.

"Maybe you weren't in the country when they first gave out tattoos," Lare speculates evenly, "and complex formulas of blood can disguise the silver in our eyes, has done so for centuries. As for your teeth... Well, you wouldn't be the first vampire to file down her fangs.

"So the only real challenge for you would be the blood, of course. But you have your ways of acquiring it, don't you, Drew? Every vampire has her way, just like every lion knows how to find the slowest gazelle. It's animal instinct, after all."

Drew holds her silence for a long moment. I have the feeling that Drew Yarrow isn't used to being pinned down, called out, or at a loss for words. Finally, she draws in a deep breath, her face deathly pale. "It's true. I am that which I loathe."

Oh, my God.

Did Mia *know*?

Drew curls her hands into fists, moving nearer to Lare. "Do you have any idea what it's like to *despise* something about yourself that cannot be changed, not ever? My whole life, I have hated what I am, what *you* are..." Her voice breaks, and she struggles to find her composure. "It...it's irrelevant now." She waves a hand in front of her face, as if brushing cobwebs aside. "I know what I have to do. I have made it my mission to assure that human beings learn the truth about the monsters they share this world with. When I'm through, no one will ever trust vampires again. The tide will shift... Vampires will go extinct. Save for one," she says, arching a brow. "And no one would ever suspect the leader of SANG to be a drinker of the blood."

Lare blinks her mirrored eyes and shakes her head sadly. "You can't repress who you really are, Drew. Vampire, human—it doesn't matter. Your *soul* defines you, not your species."

"Ah. Perhaps you'd like those pretty words engraved on your tombstone?"

Drew and Lare stare hard into one another's eyes.

Then comes a soft voice: "Drew?"

My breath hitches in my throat.

Mia. She must have crept into the room

without anyone noticing, because she's standing only a few feet away from the rest of us, wringing her hands together agitatedly, just as she had back at her apartment.

I don't know how long she's been listening, but if Mia heard Drew speak, then she knows that Drew is a vampire. Unless she always knew...

Based upon her deer-in-the-headlights expression, though, I'm guessing that she didn't, and that she does now.

Her eyes are as wide as saucers. She looks small, child-like, as she tilts her face up toward her paragon. "Drew," she says again, sounding sad, hurt. And then, as quietly as a prayer, she begs, "Please tell me it's not true. This is just part of the plan, right? You're lying to them. Drew. *Please* tell me that you're not a vampire."

Drew draws herself up to her full height. "I told you to wait for me. Go back to the room, Mia," she hisses through her false teeth.

I hold my breath.

Mia has no spine. She absorbs other people's opinions, other people's lives, as if they are her own. She believes what people tell her — until someone she admires tells her differently. She isn't a free thinker, and she doesn't want to be.

Mia does as she's told.

So right now, Mia should turn around and skulk back to the room with her tail between her legs. She should accept whatever lies Drew gives her, accept them without argument.

But...she doesn't.

"You're a vampire?" she murmurs, dazedly. She's shaking, but she doesn't back down, not even when Drew takes one menacing step toward her.

Then, suddenly, Drew's shoulders relax, and she softens her jagged features. "You heard wrong, baby," she tells Mia with a close-lipped smile. "I was only playing along—"

But Mia shakes her head, talks over Drew: "I heard the whole thing. I heard what the vampire said. Is. It. True?" she demands, stomping her foot.

Lare is still standing with her back toward me, and my heart grows wings when I see the zip ties around her wrists come loose. She keeps her hands behind her, gripping the zip ties in her palms so that they don't fall to the ground and draw attention.

"My brother was *killed* by a vampire," Mia sobs, her face pale, her lower lip trembling. "You knew that. And you... You were one of *them* all along."

Drew rolls her eyes, murmurs, "You've grown tiresome. I'll deal with you in a minute, Mia."

And Lare chooses that moment to surge forward.

I've heard rumors suggesting that

vampires are stronger than humans, and it makes sense, given the fact that humans are vampires' natural prey. Still, when Drew grabs Lare's shoulders as Lare crushes against her, trying to shove Drew down to the ground, I'm startled by what happens next.

The two women lock together. And neither budges an inch.

As the vampires wrestle, Drew snarling, Lare as silent as the grave, I feel useless, helpless.

I need to help Lare.

I shift my hands behind me, chafing my raw wrists against the rope, and I lean forward, pulling against the knots fastening me to the chair...

There's no time.

If Drew calls out for her henchmen, we're dead.

Drew realizes this at the same moment as me. "Get out here, all of you!" she shouts toward the door at the back of the warehouse, but her voice, under strain, is only a few octaves above a whisper.

Drew and Lare, locked in struggle, seem to be perfectly matched. Something has to tip the balance.

I shift my panicked gaze to Mia, who's fiddling with her phone nervously, turning it over and over in her hands as she stares, owl-eyed, in my direction. Then she sighs, taps the screen of her cell, and returns her gaze to me.

I stare back at her, nostrils flaring. She meant something to me once, I remind myself. There was goodness inside of her, a goodness that I saw, felt, wanted to hold close...

I can't believe that goodness has left her completely.

I won't believe that.

Mia narrows her brown eyes, watching me pointedly. Then: "Drew," Mia says, her voice high, whiny.

And for a split second, Drew looks toward her, losing her concentration. With lightning-fast reflexes, she catches Lare's fists in her hands as Lare shoves against her rib cage—hard.

"You lied to me, Drew," Mia says angrily, brandishing her cell. "So I called the police. It's over, babe."

"What?" Drew gasps.

The door at the back of the warehouse bursts open then, and a flood of SANG-jacketed men and women pour through.

I groan inwardly.

It's not over—not by a long shot. Because these people don't know that their fearless leader is a vampire. And it's obvious by their feral expressions that they're hellbent on aiding Drew at any cost.

But then I hear sirens... So soon?

The SANG crew pauses uncertainly, looking to Drew for orders.

"I called the cops fifteen minutes ago, when I went into the back room," Mia says quietly, flicking her gaze to me. "I realized I'd made a mistake. A big mistake. And that I didn't want Courtney to die for this. I still love her, Drew."

Drew screams hoarsely as the door to the warehouse is pounded down. As Lare shoves her away, sending Drew skidding on her back over the floor.

Then Lare stands, tall, breathing hard, her silver eyes pinned to Drew as if to make certain she doesn't attack anyone else. But Drew only scrabbles to her feet, shoulders hunched. Frantic, she tries to peel off the faux fangs affixed to her teeth.

"There she is, officers!" Mia calls out, pointing a finger in Drew's direction. "Drew Yarrow kidnapped these men and women. She lied to us all."

As uniformed policemen aim for Drew, guns drawn, Lare hurries behind me and, in a few quick gestures, unties the ropes restraining my wrists and feet. "It's okay now. It's okay," she breathes into my ear. Then she sets to work on releasing the bonds of the two men beside me.

I stretch out my arms, wincing as the blood rushes back into them. I massage my palms gingerly before pulling the tape off of my mouth and removing the gag.

Then Lare is back, and she's pressing her hot forehead against mine. There are tears on her cheeks, tears that I feel as she kisses me, her mouth warm, soft, gentle. I hold her as tightly as I can, weaving my fingers through her hair.

"I love you," she whispers, over and over. "I'm so glad you're all right. Oh, God. I love you."

I bury my face in her shoulder and inhale her scent.

"I love you, too, Lare."

The Vampire Next Door

Epilogue

Sunlight filters through the gauzy curtains, falling over my face with sweet warmth. I stretch luxuriously upon the mattress, and then I open my eyes, rising on my elbows. I take in Lare's bedroom with sleepy blinks; then I glance at the clock: eleven in the morning.

A surge of panic rises in me, but then I shake my head and sigh with relief. It's Sunday, sleep-in day. I don't have to go in to the bookstore until tomorrow. Good thing, too, because ever since the tea bar opened—offering Lare's exquisite, hand-blended teas—sales have picked up. A lot. Many of the college kids are hanging out at the shop now: to socialize, browse the shelves, study, and, of course, drink cup after cup of tea. I'm not used to so much activity at Banks' Books. But I'm definitely not complaining.

Still, I cherish this day off... Azure manages the store for me on Sundays; soon I'll have to hire another employee, to lessen the burden on us both. After David, I'm a little reluctant to hire a stranger, but it's a good problem to have, given the fact that, only a little while ago, Banks' Books was facing bankruptcy.

Last week, I finally gave Azure the raise she deserves.

I sit up in bed, and Van Helsing, who was sleeping sprawled on the floor beside me, lifts his fluffy face from his paws. He rises up slowly, deliberately, and then turns his sweet Saint Bernard face toward me, licking my cheek once.

I chuckle, ruffling the fur behind his ears. Then I slide out of bed and reach for my robe. I'm naked, and we do have neighbors, after all. I smile to myself as I tie the sash around my waist and wander down the hallway toward the living room.

And there's Lare, seated on the couch, watching the news — blatantly unconcerned about the aforementioned neighbors, because she's completely nude.

"Bonjour, beautiful," she tells me with a wide smile, holding her arms out to me. I collapse into them, kissing her deeply.

"Is this a French thing?" I tease her, gesturing to her lack of clothing.

She laughs, wrestling me easily into her lap. "Maybe," she tells me with a wink. Then she nods toward the television. "Look who it is."

The anchor on the screen is speaking about the trial of the SANG members involved in the kidnappings, slated to begin tomorrow.

"...after the leader of SANG — or Society

for the Abolishment of Nocturnal Ghouls—was arrested three months ago in relation to the kidnappings and attempted murders of four people. Numerous SANG members have been arrested since for illegal activities, including several in local government positions in Cincinnati and on the state police force. President Garcia held a nationwide press conference last week—"

"Oh, look, my favorite person," says Lare, kissing my cheek as I appear on screen.

"It's so weird, seeing yourself on television," I grimace.

They've played this news clip hundreds of times since it first aired. President Garcia invited Lare and me to the press conference herself, and who turns down the President?

"I didn't even say much." I roll my eyes as my TV twin begins to speak. "They just love showing me before they show you, to make it all titillating for the viewers, who know we're together."

"Small steps," says Lare with a wink.

The newscaster is now recounting Lare's stirring speech, and Lare's face fills the screen now, looking luminous...

I remember that day. I remember it vividly.

"...the future of vampire/human relations is poised to change, and change for the better," Lare says on the news report. "My colleagues and I are close to discovering a synthetic blood substitute that will eliminate vampires' need to drink animal or human blood entirely."

The screen now shows a montage of the magazine covers that have featured Lare since her famous speech, including *Science Today*.

"My cover girl." I kiss her again.

"...and Dr. Valeria Máille is making good on her promise," says the reporter. "After finding inspiration from an unlikely source—a book by an ancient Roman alchemist by the name of Maximinus—Dr. Máille has been able to create a blood substitute. Within a year or two, after the initial trials have been run, Valmax—named after the Roman alchemist and the scientist herself—will be available to the public, will even be available in grocery stores, effectively normalizing human/vampire interactions, so that—and I quote the doctor here—'groups like SANG will become a thing of the misguided past.'"

I grab the remote control and flick off the TV, melting against Lare's shoulder. "You may have saved the world with that potion of yours, Dr. Máille," I whisper into her ear, brushing a kiss against the pulse of her neck.

But Lare shakes her head, holding me close. "I could've never done it without my book sleuth extraordinaire."

"Hmm." I pillow my head against her chest and think for a moment, heart fluttering within my ribs. "Do you remember what you said about never being able to turn down a dare?"

Lare nods, casting a glance down at me with a soft smile.

I stand up, then, and in one smooth motion, I'm straddling her, knees on either side of her thighs. I twine my fingers in her red curls as my robe spills open.

Neighbors be damned.

"Well, I dare you to—"

But I don't get any further, because Lare claims my mouth in a kiss of mythic proportions. When we finally break away, I feel dizzy, lightheaded, and I watch as Lare's beautiful mouth slides into a satisfied smile. "You dare me to love you forever?" she asks me quietly, her head tilted to one side. She leans forward now, pressing her mouth against my heart. "I accept, *ma belle*."

I breathe out, eyelids fluttering as Lare's tender kisses trail to my breasts... "Okay, deal," I laugh lightly.

Lare works a line of gentle kisses over my chest. "*Je t'aime...*" she murmurs against me.

"I love you," I tell her fiercely. And then again, "I love you."

I'll never be able to speak those words to her enough. Loving Lare is the truest thing I know.

"So, Courtney, what do you want to do

today?" Lare considers me as I arch over her, as I bring my head down towards hers.

"Oh, I don't know. I can think of a couple of things I'd like to do..."

Laughing, vampire teeth bared, Lare glides her hands over my shoulders, pushing back my robe.

"But I'm going to start with you," I grin at her.

And I kiss her, and every day, I know, we will begin the rest of our lives together in just this way: sweetly, softly, with a kiss.

The End

Authors' Note

A funny thing happened on one of the very last days that we were editing *The Vampire Next Door* for publication.

We almost died.

We were coming home from a small trip to the craft store. You know those trips—a quick little car ride to pick up a tiny, inconsequential thing while you're thinking about it, just to get yourself out of the house. We'd both been working so hard on *The Vampire Next Door* that we really did want to get out of the house, and we needed a small thing from the craft store...so we figured: why not go?

We were driving home, driving through a green light, when a driver ran the red, hitting us in the side. He came so fast, out of nowhere, and we were propelled instantly into oncoming traffic. We ricocheted off of oncoming traffic, spinning several times until all was still. The front of the car was smashed in, the airbags were deployed, and the sides of the car were so smashed, we couldn't open the doors to get out.

A lot of things happen when you're in a car accident so severe that the car has to be swept off of the road in pieces. For one, your life really *does* flash in front of your eyes. For another, the most important things in your life become even more evident than they already were.

The only thing that either of us could think of was the other. The only thing we could say was "I love you" and "it's okay," and "baby" as we called out to each other in the spinning maelstrom of the accident.

The police couldn't believe that we were able to walk out of the car. And we did, sustaining minor injuries.

We were alive.

Writing *The Vampire Next Door* together was an exhilarating, amazing ride from start to finish. Ever since we'd gotten together, well over a decade ago now, we talked about writing a book together. We're lifelong writers, and have written *so many books*, but we'd just never gotten around to writing one together, as much as we wanted to.

In those bleak, dark moments during the accident, when we didn't know whether we would live or die, all we could do was call out to one another, hold each other's hand and hope that things were going to be all right.

When we were finally out of the wreck, when we could finally hold each other, kiss each other, embrace one another and make certain the other was okay...one of the first things we said was: "at least we'd written that book together." We were so glad, in those moments, that something we'd wanted to do for our whole lives was the thing we'd accomplished.

We loved writing this story together.

And we're incredibly grateful to be alive. One of the most important things we took away from the accident was to never, ever put off that thing you really want to do. We each got to write a book with our favorite author. That's pretty spectacular. We're so glad we made the time to do it, that we had such an amazing ride writing together along the way.

We're so grateful that you've read *The Vampire Next Door*. We hope you enjoyed it as much as we enjoyed writing it together.

We're lucky to be alive. But then, every day, for every single one of us, is a gift. Thank you for taking some small time out of your own life to enjoy our story.

        Natalie Vivien & Bridget Essex
        April, 2015

Made in the USA
San Bernardino, CA
07 June 2016